D1287564

THE WHITE APACHE

They called Drury a murdering renegade who led the Apaches against his own people. Royal, the rock-hard manhunter, had finally got the drop on him. The best Drury could hope for when—if—they got him back to Tucson was that the hangman wouldn't bungle the job. But they didn't call him the White Apache for nothing, and an awful lot could happen along treacherous mountain trails.

In the end, Drury had two choices. He could make a break for it and become what they said he was—a turncoat killer. Or he could stay and prove that he was a better man than any of them.

THE WHITE APACHE

L. L. Foreman

GUNSMOKE

This hardback edition 2008
by BBC Audiobooks Ltd
by arrangement with
Golden West Literary Agency

ISBN 978 1 405 68154 4

British Library Cataloguing in Publication Data available.

Printed and bound in Great Britain by
Antony Rowe Ltd., Chippenham, Wiltshire

CHAPTER ONE

Four passengers, one of them handcuffed, climbed aboard the Tucson-bound stage at Cometi. They settled themselves on the hard leather seats inside the coach, resigned to bear the discomfort of a rough journey, not sorry to leave that drab bordertown. Even the man in handcuffs breathed a sigh of relief, though going to his doom. The outside air, oppressively hot, was fresh compared to that of the stifling cell, Cometi's one-cell jail, a sweatbox.

A squad of Arizona Rangers, iron men heavily armed, with merciless eyes, stood in the bare street to see the stage off. Being reformed wildlings for the most part, Rangers brought sternness to their duty, a pitiless intolerance of outlaws. The zeal of converts.

Their sergeant spoke final words of strict caution to the U.S. deputy marshal in the coach, who had taken the manacled man, a federal prisoner, off the Rangers' hands and would escort him to Tucson for trial. "Keep your eye sharp on him, Mr. Royal, he's dangerous!"

"I can manage."

"I'm sure you can." The sergeant hoped so, privately allowing a twinge of misgiving. The federal law officer, cold as ice and clipped of speech, appeared to be extremely efficient but he wasn't familiar with this south Arizona country. "Just don't give him an inch."

The stage carried only a dab of unimportant mail, the run being a boondock operation, but the mail contract required an armed guard. From his perch beside the driver, the guard called down, "I'll give the marshal a hand if he needs it!" He raised his shotgun. "This'd fix that Injun-lovin' devil, eh?"

One of the other two passengers in the coach, a cattle buyer from Texas, ran a marble-eyed stare over the prisoner. "Count me in," he announced. "Be a pleasure to kill him!"

The fourth passenger, a whiskey drummer on the downdrift, fumblingly brushed his shabby bowler hat with his coatsleeve. Shaky, a beaten victim of his own wares, he avoided meeting anyone's eyes for fear of meeting contempt.

Screeching his yell, the driver cracked the whip and the coach lunged forward. Royal—Mr. Royal, U.S. deputy marshal, gave the squad of Arizona Rangers a cool good-bye nod. In return, the sergeant touched his hat perfunctorily, a slouchy gesture toward politeness, nothing more. No warm regard there.

The prisoner, Jim Drury, understood that, and because something else was called for, or for the hell of it, he raised his manacled hands, waggling his fingers in farewell. The sergeant nodded slightly, taking off his hat, holding it before him in both hands as if at a passing funeral.

Well, that was right, Jim Drury thought. My funeral. Royal, this chill and bloodless man facing me across the seat, watching my every move, will see me hang in Tucson. The Rangers in Cometi weren't kind, far from it—me being Drury—but at least they were human. This man is inhuman. A stiff-backed ramrod.

He had disliked Royal on sight, when Royal had arrived on the downstage the day before and correctly presented the federal requisition—signed by high rank —for the prisoner. Drury sensed that the dislike was mutual. Antipathy, silent but positive, burned between them like the reaction of mutually corrosive metals.

They hated each other. Not for the surface reason that one was a rigid lawman and the other an outlaw. Underneath, Drury thought, we're alike. I could be wearing his badge. Grace of God, or joke of Satan, which? The son-of-a-bitch could be wearing my handcuffs, but for the twists of circumstances that shape our lives. Oh, well—

It was early summer and already brutally hot by day. Dry washouts slammed the coach, and baked ruts slewed it creaking from side to side behind the heedless team of half-broken broncs. The stageline company, a struggling outfit, scrimped on its horses and equipment, forcing the drivers to make do and get by as best they could. On his high seat the driver rode the bumps, cursing the team and the road. Beside him the shotgun guard cursed his job.

Toward Pozo Blanco the road narrowed into a rising cut, with steep hills on one side and a sheer drop-off on the other. Here and there cave-ins had broken away chunks of the road, pinching it narrower, barely leaving space for the stagecoach to pass. At times the off side seemed to hang out over the drop-off, the wheels only inches from the edge.

The whiskey drummer looked through the glassless side window, looked down the long slope and hurriedly plucked a bottle from his sample case. He drank deeply, shuddering, before offering the bottle half-heartedly to the cattle buyer.

His offer went curtly rejected, the cattle buyer being a hard-shell Texan prejudiced against anyone wearing a bowler hat—always excepting roundup cooks, dour individualists who wore anything they damn well pleased and brooked no criticism.

The drummer then motioned his bottle at U.S. Deputy Marshal Royal, though knowing beforehand it would be refused there, too. "It smooths the road," he muttered.

The federal officer declined. He didn't suggest that his prisoner could possibly use a stiff drink to smooth *his* road. Nor did the drummer, who, at last defiant of contempt, tipped the bottle back to his mouth. "Smooths the road," he repeated.

The road played him false. A chuckhole bounced the coach in a jarring thank-you-ma'am and more whiskey sloshed into his mouth than he could handily swallow. He choked and coughed, sputtering it down his front.

The Texan split a sour, meager grin, then gazed angrily out at the broad view of bare lands southward, desert country. He was angry because this year had gone bad. His buying trip was a failure, a waste of time and expense. The small cowmen along the border— hardscrabble cowmen he had done business with in previous years—were now demanding hard cash on the nail for their cows, no promissory notes and handshake agreements.

He didn't have that kind of ready money. His annual spring operation involved shaping up a trail herd from small gatherings, on credit, and delivering it at the northern markets where he knew the tricks of obtaining top prices. He was honest within his lights, had always returned and paid off his obligations, carving a thick whack of profit for himself. But the whole operation took months, as any cowman knew.

Why their refusal this year? It was as if the border folks expected a crushing disaster and placed their faith only in quick cash, gold. No trust in the future. As if they sensed something in the wind. But they wouldn't speak of it. The border folks were a close-mouthed lot: Mexican, Indian, and *americano* loners, extremely reticent, never breathing a word that might spark a deadly feud. It baffled the Texan. He put no stock in reasonless instinct.

The prisoner, Drury, spoke for the first time since the stage had pulled out of Cometi. He had appeared to be dozing in his blackened, hardworn buckskins, Indian dress, or sunk in a lethargy of resignation. A black growth of piratical beard, the growth of two years, enhanced his air of dangerousness, of violence. He was a large man, bone-lean, whose age was difficult to guess, for above the beard his face looked ravaged, with deeply socketed eyes, muscled brows, a jutting nose.

"Marshal," he murmured, "we're in for trouble."

Quiet though his words were, they reached the Texan on the opposite seat. The Texan leaned forward, the nameless fear of the border dwellers springing alive and itching his mind. "What trouble? What kind?"

The whiskey drummer washed his abused throat with another swallow from the bottle, careless now of any trouble.

Drury closed his eyes as if to think better, presently opening them: slate-gray eyes, opaque. "Ambush ahead. Apaches, I think likely."

"Friends of yours!" The Texan drew his gun from its holster. He rested it, a heavy, long-barreled man-stopper, between his knees. "Marshal! If he tries a break you shoot him, or I will!"

The U.S. deputy marshal also drew his gun, calmly and without haste. "If you attempt to shoot my prisoner, I'll have to shoot you!" he stated. Fresh to the raw country, yet he was quite sure of himself.

"Dammit, he says there's an ambush—"

"How would he know? He can't see the road ahead. He's riding backward."

9

"Could be he planned an ambush with some of his Apaches!"

"Not a chance. He's been under close watch night and day since his arrest. Every minute. The Rangers were aware of that danger. They took every precaution." Royal looked directly at Drury. "There's no earthly way you could know of any ambush. You're bluffing!"

He dipped a glance at the handcuffs. He knew by repute of Drury's immense strength, but the handcuffs had been fashioned to order by a master smithy. The man wasn't born who could snap that tempered steel.

Drury's opaque eyes blanked eerily. "I just know."

The Texan shifted uneasily on his seat. He spat forcefully out the window, trying to restore self-confidence, and declared, "In Texas, by God, we've got a short way with renegades!"

"This isn't Texas," Royal reminded him. "He'll hang, make no mistake about that. Now put away your gun, or I'll have to arrest you."

"Arrest me for what?"

"For threatening interference to a federal officer."

"Hell of a thing!" The bristling Texan holstered his big gun. "Protecting a goddam—"

"He's a federal prisoner in my charge."

They rode on then in silence until Drury said, "You'd be wise to persuade the driver to turn off on the Picacho fork along here."

"What's in Picacho?" Royal inquired drily.

"Nothing much. A Mexican village."

"Off our route, is it?"

"Some. But—"

"It's a trick, Marshal!" interrupted the Texan. "I bet some of his Apache pals are skulking around Picacho. That's where the ambush would be."

"Don't worry, we're not going there," Royal said. He rolled a cigarette, passed it over to Drury and scratched a a match alight for him.

It surprised Drury. In a moment, though, he recognized it as the coldest kind of charity, an act deliberately intended to impress upon him his inferior position. It was meant to symbolize the harsh fact that he was a prisoner, completely under Royal's control, dependent upon Royal for small favors.

He inhaled deeply. His first smoke in days. The Arizona Rangers had shown no kindness but neither had they offered him the humiliating insult of cold charity.

The smoke tasted bitter. Drury spat the cigarette out and crushed it under his foot.

Watching him do it, Royal smiled faintly, aware of Drury's impotent resentment. Their stares met. The law officer's gaze hardened, mutely informing the prisoner that he as the underdog must watch his step, take what was given to him, eat humble pie.

Behind his blanked stare Drury was thinking, You'll never get me to Tucson alive, damn you—

CHAPTER TWO

The attack came on the brow of a long, curving highrise where anyone could predict with certainty that the driver would have to halt his team for a breather. The ambushing Apaches opened fire after the brakes were set.

Shot in the first volley, the driver died while bending to tie his lines, he having figured on taking time out to fill and light his pipe. The shotgun guard, Zorn, jumped to the ground, glaring wildly about, but of course the Apaches weren't showing themselves this soon in the game. A second blast of rifles lashed down from the high bank overlooking the road. Zorn fell alongside the horses that were threshing in panic.

The whiskey drummer, clutching the depleted bottle, stuck his head out of the coach. "Jesus, they're on top of us!" he mouthed thickly before a bullet smacked him.

The Texan blared at Drury, "Call 'em off or I'll kill you dead, you—"

"You won't!" Royal said over a drawn gun.

Rifle fire flayed the stalled coach from above, smashing through the roof boards. The horses lay kicking in tangled harness, and Apache yells of triumph began shrilling. Swearing, the Texan called him a damn fool Yankee jackass.

He plunged out, shooting up the bank, bound to prove that one good Texas man made more than a match for any skulking redskins. A hail of bullets from brush-cover promptly corrected him, though he didn't live to meditate on the lesson.

"Marshal," said Drury, "take these handcuffs off!"

"Not till I hand you over at Tucson."

"We'll never reach Tucson. You need me now."

"Like I need a rattlesnake!" Royal snapped. He slid out of the off-side door. "Stay where you are."

"And get shot?"

"It's your own doing."

With the blind side of the coach for partial protection, Royal took quick aim and fired up into a rustling mesquite. His shot drew a stifled howl and next a furious blast of return fire. Touching a hand to his chest, he leaned against the coach, face lowered. He had exposed himself for only an instant.

Drury eased out and joined him. He searched into Royal's pockets. Royal struck at him clumsily. "Damn you, don't—" he coughed. He had dropped his gun. Reaching down for it, he sank to his knees and hung there clasping onto the rear wheel for support.

Drury found what he sought, the slender key to the handcuffs. With some difficulty he fitted it into the lock, sprang open the handcuffs, and tossed them from him as if the hated things burned.

He spread his hands apart, luxuriating in liberty after the intolerable days of captivity cooped in the Cometi jail—the adobe cell an oven half the time; watched ceaselessly by taciturn guards whose eyes expressed the chill revulsion of men looking into a cage at a beast.

An Apache bullet from above hit the handcuffs lying in the road, reminding him that his liberty was narrowly limited. He was the only man of the stagecoach party left alive and unhurt.

Royal, turning painfully to sit with his back to the wheel, said to him, "You seem to have taught your Apache friends a few things!"

"How's that?"

"Apaches are poor shots, I've been told. Unreliable. Hit-and-run fighters. Not these. These are sharp-shooters. Thanks to your teaching, I suppose!"

Drury didn't reply, having nothing worth saying in argument. Newcomers were apt to pick up half-truths from townies who got their information from hearsay. Under conditions of their own choosing, Apaches were fighting fiends. To their minds it was only sensible to fade off when the odds turned against them.

From the rate of gunfire, as well as the yipping, Drury put the number of Apaches at probably eight. The warriors as a rule preferred going in compact groups on the warpath—raiding parties scouting for blood and loot.

Eight warriors armed with Winchester .45 repeaters.

He considered, however, that these warriors could very well be an advance-party of the main force. They could be feelers for the mass attack, and therefore in touch with other war parties. This was the Red Year, proclaimed by Geronimo and his subchiefs. The year when the Apaches would rise and drive all the White-faces out of the Southwest, the ancient Apache land where for ages the Apaches had ruled as masters.

Drury picked up the gun that had belonged to the Texas cattle buyer—the would-be cattle buyer, now dead. The gun was a heavy Dragoon .44 cap-and-ball, converted into a center-fire cartridge gun like thousands in the West. It felt right to Drury's hand. He had carried just such a gun in days gone by, when he was simply a white man among white men, before infamy had clouded him.

He unbuckled and stripped off the Texan's gun belt, hung with a sheathed Bowie knife as well as the holster and looped shells. He strapped the belt on himself, breathing a heartfelt, "Ah!—"

His dull resignation dissipated. He was free and armed.

But the Dragoon .44 gun wasn't good enough against the eight Apache braves. Or seven, if Royal's shot had scored hard. The ambushing Apaches possessed good rifles, traded for at high cost, or stolen. Winchester .45 repeaters. Better rifles than those issued to the Army.

The mail guard, Zorn, lay close by the slain team of the stagecoach. He had fallen on his shotgun, pinning it under him. He was in plain sight of the Apaches. His shotgun was a double-barrel 12-bore loaded with buckshot. Drury decided he would have that fearsome weapon to go with the Dragoon gun.

Stretching flat on the ground, he reached forward and grasped Zorn's nearest ankle. He tugged Zorn toward him, inches at a time, having to resettle himself after each effort.

The movement of the body renewed the Apache gunfire. Bullets lashed the body. If any spark of life had remained in Zorn, it certainly was quenched now. Zorn was very dead.

U.S. Deputy Marshal Royal looked on wonderingly at Drury's actions. He couldn't understand why Drury didn't call out to the Apaches and show himself. Drury knew all the Apaches. They all knew him. He was bloodbrother to the Apaches. He was the White Apache, dreaded warchief who dealt such cruelty to captives that his braves stood in awe of him.

Yet—And yet—Here was this, the incredible thing. The unbelievable action.

The bullet-riddled body of Zorn, dragged by Drury, dragged the shotgun with it. With a final tug Drury drew the shotgun to within his reach. He pulled it free, then rummaged through the pockets of dead Zorn's jacket and took the spare shells, four.

He knelt in the shelter of the coach, taking stock and considering his next move.

The Apache marauders knew now, of course, that they had wasted their precious ammunition on a corpse. They knew that one of the ambushed whites was still living, still able to fight and that he had secured the mail guard's shotgun. Which meant they wouldn't risk a rushing onslaught. Not by daylight, anyway, against that feared weapon.

No, they would wait for darkness. Then creep down, circle him, hem him in tight. Meantime, fray his nerves. Make him spend his ammunition, such as he had. They throated their sharp cries, wolf-yappings intended to put shuddering horrors into the lone defender.

They hadn't long to wait.

Drury glanced toward the lowering sun. A scant hour of daylight was left. He drew his knife—the dead cattle buyer's Texas Bowie—and tested its edge with his thumb. It was sharp as a razor. Meanwhile, his eyes strayed to Royal, to Royal's gun.

Propped against the coach wheel, Royal raised his gun, having to use both hands to steady it, and asked, "Do you aim to take my scalp with that knife?"

Drury slid the knife back into its sheath. "No," he said absently. His mind was intently occupied with what he had to do. "I'm just checking over my weapons before I leave."

Royal watched him eject empty shells from the Dragoon pistol and reload its chambers from the cartridge belt. "You're off to join your Apache friends, eh?"

"I'll be back."

"With your Apaches! To enjoy the sport after they capture me alive, eh?"

A dark flush spread over Drury's face. He felt the heat of it. He stared fixedly at the wounded lawman. It was a strange look, weighted with brooding menace and yet also a bleak kind of pity. He raised his head and sent out a call, the throaty pitch of it an exact imitation of the Apaches' yapping. The words he uttered were in a language unknown to Royal.

"Bitra 'shte lo!"

Between the blind side of the stagecoach and the edge of the road there was an open space visible to the sharpshooters above on the bank. Below the road's edge the steep slope studded sparsely with mesquite and fallen rocks, sheered far down to still another drop-off that promised sure death if a man survived the first fall.

Intrigued by Drury's call, the Apaches broke off their firing and yapping to listen together for further words.

They're not sure of who I am, Drury thought. He assumed they had begun stalking the stagecoach at about the time he had tried to warn Royal. Fleet afoot and soundless, they had ghosted on ahead and picked this perfect spot to lay their ambush.

He cast a measuring glance at Royal and his unsteadily pointing gun. Royal, correctly reading the glance snapped, "I'd be justified in killing you!"

"You'd have to shoot me in the back because here I go!"

From his muscle-tensed crouch Drury leaped the open space to the edge of the road and dropped feet-first over it. Royal's shot followed a shade late and too high. His wound had slowed his reflexes.

The Apaches, confused by Drury's Indian call had momentarily ceased firing, which gave him the instant he needed to vacate the dwindling shelter of the stage-coach and quit the road.

He landed, sliding, on his back. Arms outspread to

avoid a disastrous roll, he dug in his heels, attempting to slow his fall and guide it toward a rock, a mesquite, any obstruction. Stones and loosened shale cascaded after him. He smashed into a stunted mesquite and clung to it, half-buried, while the surface avalanche that he had caused passed him by.

He was a long way down the slope, fearfully close to the lower drop-off. His descent had been fast, tearing his clothes to rags and his skin to shreds. But he had kept hold of the shotgun. He heard the Apaches shooting again. Their yapping sounded fiercely angry. They wouldn't lie waiting for darkness, not now, knowing that the stagecoach sheltered only a wounded man, who had killed one of them and must pay for it. They had to get him before he too cheated them with an escape-trick. Royal's gun thudded a single report, heavy among the sharp crack of rifles. The man was still alive and putting up a forlorn fight.

Get moving, Drury commanded himself, time's shrinking.

He crawled free of the mesquite and began easing along the slope, picking his way foot by foot, shunning humps where he might line himself up for an Apache bullet. The shotgun was an awkward encumbrance in places requiring both hands, but he kept it at the cost of skinned knuckles and elbows. Twice he went into a perilous slide, losing ground.

When he got beyond the curve of the road he clawed directly upward until, near the road, caution ordered a pause. Firing continued spasmodically in the vicinity of the stagecoach. The Apaches evidently had plenty of ammunition to spend. They had counted him out, he hoped, believing he couldn't have survived his leap down the slope without crippling himself. They were firing to hold Royal pinned to cover, while they snaked down closer. Not to kill him. To take him alive.

He heard Royal's gun once more. Probably triggered at random in a faint hope of staving off the creeping advance. Royal knew what capture entailed, if he knew little else about Apache habits. He knew they were coming down for him.

Scrambling the last few feet, Drury darted across the road. The rising curve hid him. He ran into the brush of the upper bank, where he took a breath before climbing higher in a wide half-circle, a route aimed at bringing him above and behind the ambushers. He was as fleet afoot and silent as they, for the fine art of deadly brush-stalking had been taught him by Apaches.

CHAPTER THREE

Spread flat on a shelf of rimrock, the young brave appeared to be meditating, possibly sulking because the older warriors had posted him there in the rear as a lookout—thankless task—while they pressed onward. He wore a loincloth and headband, nothing else except an old Mexican bandoleer which, however, bulged with greased shells for his good Henry repeater.

Once in a while he fired down at the stranded stagecoach but only to inform the warriors that he wasn't asleep at his post. He fretfully amused himself by spanging bullets off a handrail. Fine shooting, though a prodigal waste.

Where had they obtained such rifles, such abundance of ammunition? Drury shrugged, dismissing the question. There were always conscienceless traders. The Apaches, gangsters of the border, had long prepared for this year. Plunder for arms. Horses, cattle, household goods and bits of jewelry, slaves sold to Comanches—

Instinct jerked the young brave suddenly taut. He squirmed around. His eyes widened enormously at sight of the tattered and bloody apparition, the gaunt, bearded face, the flash of a blade. He whipped his rifle over and opened his mouth to scream an alarm to the warriors below.

The sweeping stroke of the Bowie upthrust to the hilt just beneath his rib cage. He sank without a moan, mouth and eyes still wide. His muscles quivered briefly, then his body lay slack and sunken like half-melted wax, the skin seeming to lose at once its hue and texture.

Drury withdrew the knife gravely, taking no pride in the necessary kill. He wiped it on the youth's loincloth. "Too bad, youngster. Well—" He shrugged away regret, remembering how viciously murderous were the young braves who itched to gain prestige. Dangerous as kid gunmen on the prod, big behind a gun. There wasn't much difference. Blood prestige: the count of the slain.

He prowled onward down the bank, using every scrap of cover, searching for the forward attackers. Soon they would rush the stagecoach, if they didn't first send back to discover why the young lookout's rifle had fallen silent. He had very little time.

A pair of wolf-faced warriors, black-striped, slipped through the brush. They preciously cuddled their rifles and held with elbows the slung bandoleers to guard from telltale slapping. The Apaches had learned that firearms require care—barrels must be clean, breeches oiled. They persisted in brass-studding the stocks and butts—a foolish vanity, for the brass nails often split the wood, which then had to be tightly wire-bound to keep from coming apart.

One of the two warriors turned his head querulously to the other, who veered over to him. They paused together, whispering, scowling backward up the bank. Something had twanged an instinct, rung a bell. Not a noise. Drury was as soundless as they. But still they sensed a menace.

Drury fired the shotgun. He aimed between—to the left of one, to the other's right—and scored on both. The spread of buckshot, at that range, tore into them. It whirled them facing each other. The second barrel he discharged higher. Their slug-pitted heads lolled and they both fell.

He reloaded the shotgun fast, keeping the Dragoon

.44 pistol in reserve—he'd need that in the pinch. The remaining Apaches, nearest to the stagecoach, would now lie alertly waiting for him, aware of an unexpected rear attack.

He crawled on, careful to set no stones tumbling. In minutes he glimpsed a man whose scars and paint proclaimed tribal fame. A seasoned warrior, a leader. He resembled Chato, whom Drury had met and known in Mexico. But Chato was a Chiricahua chieftain. Had the Chiricahuas joined the Apache uprising? If so, what of the Jicarillos, Mescalleros, all the Apache tribes? All on the warpath?

Grimacing, eyes glinting, the seasoned warrior sensed he was being stalked. Uncertainly, he swung his rifle, pointing it this way and that, seeking a target. A slight rustle in a juniper patch fixed his attention. Drury inched forward the shotgun, squeezed trigger and the warrior slumped, no longer resembling Chief Chato or anyone else.

Three of them were left, Drury estimated, if his original guess of eight had been correct. He had got four. Royal had got one.

The three would be tough to beat if they stayed in cover. On the other hand, maybe not. The toughest of them leaned to the fight-and-run tradition. Not for Apaches the whooping charge of the Sioux and Cheyenne, feathered lances and war bonnets fluttering. Apaches didn't indulge in such gaudy heroics. They were realists, down-to-earth opportunists, waging war not for glory but for profit, hatred, vengeance, at minimum damage to themselves.

The sun sank low before he ended his search. The three Apaches lay motionless under a clump of juniper. Waiting and watching, they didn't exchange a whisper.

Their enemy was a crafty devil. They were on the defensive, an unfamiliar and uneasy position for Apaches.

He would have missed spotting them if a shaft of the slanting sun hadn't played on a bare buttock. Their silent stillness implied bitter respect for the stalking foe and his shotgun. The stagecoach was forgotten for the time being.

He blasted two loads of buckshot into the clump of juniper. He dropped the shotgun, having no time to reload it and drew the Dragoon .44 for a follow-up.

One of the three sprang upright with an unearthly yell, clutching his buttocks. His whoop shattered the stillness. His companions jumped up and fled, crashing through brush. The buttocks-torn man hopped after them. Drury let them go.

He holstered the pistol. Descending the bank to the road, he stepped around the stagecoach to its blind side. There he confronted the muzzle of Royal's gun.

Royal held the cocked gun aimed at him. Slowly lowering it, he said, "I thought it was an Indian coming."

"The Indians," Drury said, "are gone."

He ducked into the stagecoach. He took a full bottle from the whiskey drummer's sample case. He rummaged into the dead Texan's warbag.

"Robbing the dead?" Royal called.

Drury backed out of the stagecoach, stuffing his pockets. "We've got a hard row to hoe. Three Apaches got away. They'll be back with another bunch. What I've taken could be useful to us on the long dodge."

"You killed the rest of them?" Royal asked, astonished.

"What the hell d'you think I was doing up there? Playing tiddlywinks with 'em?"

"But your own people—Apaches—"

"Let it drop," Drury said. He hoisted Royal up off the ground by his armpits. "Can you use your legs?"

"Can try."

"Try damn hard!"

Royal pulled distrustfully away from him. "What's your game? What are you trying to do?"

Drury caught the law officer by his arm, steadying him from a toppling stagger. "Dammit, man, I'm trying to keep you out of the Apaches' hands!"

"Why? I'm trying to take you in for trial—for murder and God knows what else! Why should you help me, you of all people?"

"I'll take you to Tucson if I can—to hang!"

"Fair warning, not that I need it. Get a move on, or I'll clout you cold and lug you out of here!"

The question had gone unanswered.

They made a halt in a gravelly hollow sheltered by hills barren of any growth except the mesquite. Drury let Royal down—he had been half-carrying him—and scrabbled up a few sticks of deadwood.

With his hands and a heel he scooped out a hole in the gravel and lit a small fire in it, after which he offered Royal the now nearly empty bottle.

Royal drank sparingly, shuddering at the raw bite of whiskey at his parched throat. He returned the bottle to Drury, nodding his thanks. His shuddering merged into shivering and he drew closer to the fire, his weakened body unable to combat the chilly night air. The temperature, as always, had dropped quickly after sundown, the arid earth and dry atmosphere not retaining the day's intense heat.

The cloudless sky, deep indigo blue-black, coldly flaunted brilliant ice-chip stars. In the vast dead silence the snap and crackle of the mesquite fire sounded shockingly loud.

"Aren't you afraid of the fire being seen?" Royal asked.

"There are no Apaches hereabouts," Drury answered him. "Nobody. We're safe here for a while."

Safe for a few hours, he thought. Should be hurrying on, taking advantage of the dark. Like most Indians, the Apaches flinched from darkness. A matter of religion; superstition in their case. The great *Wakan* abhorred the spirits of those who died in darkness. Unless on a moonlight night. This night was moonless so far. Superstition? It made sense of a kind.

But, Drury meditated, Royal was getting too weak to travel. I'm getting worn out, lugging him along, he thought.

Drury's eyes were bloodshot between thickened lids. He needed food, drink, sleep. Royal needed a doctor, badly. Perhaps it was already too late. The rifle bullet had torn into his lungs. Internal bleeding. Infection.

"How can you be sure we're safe here?" Royal persisted. "We couldn't see them in this dark. And God knows we'd never hear them."

"I covered our tracks." Covered their tracks for a night and a day, and part of this night. Backtrailing, brushing out signs, trudging onward again. A laborious progress of a few miles.

"Yes, but can Apache trackers be stumped?"

"They can be stalled. For a few hours, I said. We'll be gone before they get here. I'll know if they're coming."

"How will you know?" Royal raised his face from the tiny fire, teeth still chattering, lips blue. "How?"

25

"Same way I knew they were stalking the stage-coach."

"Animal instinct?" Royal put emphasis on the first word, making it anything but complimentary.

Drury took off his coat. "Call it what you like. You don't have it, that's sure." He wrapped his coat, the Texan's coat, over Royal, and went foraging for more deadwood.

Feeding scraps to the fire, he said, as if teaching an elementary lesson to a greenhorn, "When you're trying to trap wild horses, you've got to be careful not to think about the trap you've set for 'em. If you're too anxious, too eager, the horses catch on. They don't have to see the trap. They sense it and shy off."

"A sense of unseen danger?" Royal questioned.

Drury nodded. "Unseen, but felt. Good mustangers take it into account. So do Indians. Animal instinct. Lots of wild animals have it. That's how they survive."

"And men?" Royal huddled under the coat. "Indians, yes, especially Apaches—but white men?"

"Some. A few. Trappers. Scouts. And men long hunted—outlaws. They acquire it, more or less. Some, though, are born with it—that strong feeling—that sure knowing when enemies and danger come near. You haven't got it, Royal."

"You have! Did you aquire it as a hunted outlaw?"

"No, I was born with it." Somberly, almost to himself, Drury added, "It's done me more harm than good."

"We could have strayed into several Apache bands," Royal conceded, "and I wouldn't have known."

"That's right. Without me, you'd be slowly roasting alive over an Apache pit-fire, lawman!"

"How long is it since the attack on the stagecoach? I don't seem to remember—"

"Forty-some hours. Part of the time," Drury said, "you've been out of your head. You've got a bad wound. I'm trying to get you to Tucson, to a doctor."

Royal asked his irritatingly constant question: "Why,"

"To show you I'm the better man!"

Royal threw off the coat. "You may know this god-forsaken country better than I do but I can make my way anywhere!" He coughed rackingly, chest-deep, bringing up blood, dribbling it down his once-white shirt. "Go to hell, renegade!"

"Hell's yours if I go," Drury said. "The Apaches are up, all their tribes. A total uprising. You wouldn't last the night. Put that coat back on and take another drink."

Weakened by his loss of blood, Royal obeyed, asking muddledly, "D'you know for a fact the Apaches—"

"I do," Drury said. "I lived among Apaches for two years. I know their language, their customs. The Apache uprising is now. It's been set for this year. Set by someone who knows that the Army is understrength. The Army this year is discharging its old soldiers, replacing them with green recruits—thanks to penny-pinching politicians. Old soldiers earn up to eighty dollars a month. Recruits draw sixteen."

"Are you the someone who tipped off the Apaches—"

"No. I have information of the Apache uprising. I brought warning of it. But in Cometi—that stinking little bordertown—who'd have guessed it? A squad of Arizona Rangers, quartering there."

"Your animal instinct—?"

"It didn't work. Because they weren't expecting me. Didn't have their minds on me. And I wasn't looking for them there. Don't you understand?"

"I think I do. The trap wasn't set for you. It was just a—a happenstance. So you weren't on guard."

"You're learning," Drury said. "I walked barefaced into the Rangers. Not a chance to back out. They were as surprised as I was. They knew me right away—my description on the wanted bills. The clothes I wore. My height, six-three. I tried to give those Rangers warning of the Apache uprising. You think they'd listen to me—*me?*"

Royal spread his shaking hands to the fire. "No," he responded reflectively. "Nor would I."

"Because of prejudice?"

"Partly. And partly because a prophet is never honored in his own country. Particularly a prophet of misfortune."

"That's a fact," Drury agreed. "If you predict misfortune, and it comes, you're liable to take the blame for it. That's happened to me more than once."

"In olden days the bearer of bad news often got his head chopped off," Royal remarked. "You speak like a man who's had a trifle of education in your past."

"A trifle is right."

"Me too."

They looked measuringly at each other across the fire, both of them admitting reluctantly, grudgingly, a thin thread, very thin, of possible kinship.

"I'm a burden to you," Royal said. "Don't deny it! I can't even walk straight without help."

"Who's denying it? Sure you're a burden. Tomorrow I'll have to carry you. And the day after."

"If we're alive."

"Right. The odds are against it," Drury allowed, "due to thirst as well as Apaches. We've got a considerable way ahead before there's any water I know of. And some Apaches might be there."

"The cursed Apaches! Why can't they settle down, like other tribes?"

"Well, they've got their grievances. They've been shoved around a long time, couple of hundred years or more, hunted by government troops—Spanish, then Mexican, then American. They hold the grudge. This was their country."

Royal shook his head, unconvinced, but too hurt and weak to argue. "Why don't you abandon me? You might be able to save yourself, alone."

"I'm not about to do it."

"Why not?"

Suddenly exasperated, Drury exclaimed, "Always that goddam 'why' from you! Shut up and get some rest!"

Royal spread trembling hands to the fire. "Are you trying to prove something?"

"I told you what I'm trying to prove."

"How far to that waterhole?"

"No waterhole. It's a seep-spring in a cave. Cold, fresh water. Lord, I can taste it!" Drury sucked for saliva. His parched mouth refused it to him.

"How far?" Royal repeated.

"About ten miles, if I've got our bearings figured right."

"I can't make it. You know I can't, don't you?"

"Yeah. So, like I said, I'll have to carry you."

"You're placing me in your debt," Royal said, "because you hate my guts. But there must be a limit to debt. A limit to everything." His mind had begun wandering like the mind of a drunken man, diamond-sharp

29

and at the same time fogged, figuring turgid paths of philosophy.

"Sure," Drury said. "A limit to hate, too. Let's kill the fire and mosey on.—"

CHAPTER FOUR

Dazzling sunshine outside accentuated the cool gloom within the cave, where the steady drip-drip of water made a tinkling sound like that of a toy bell.

Before it reached the cave's sun-baked mouth the trickle sank into the ground. It left a permanent damp spot, from the seep-spring, nothing that a passing rider was likely to notice.

Black remains of cookfires gave evidence that the cave, once in a while, had been used as a campsite in the past. By wandering Indians. By outlaws in lonely hiding. This far off the common trails, nobody else was likely to use it or even know of its existence.

Royal, face sunken, eyes closed, lay stretched on the ground. It was difficult to tell whether he was asleep or had lost consciousness again. He had somehow thrown off fever but his breathing was ragged and shallow. His grip on life was slipping.

Around midday he opened his eyes. Gazing up at the roof of the cave he said quite clearly, "Thanks, Drury. For staying with me. How long's it been?"

For long periods he had floated in a haze of dreams, vague reveries, recalling and reliving his past life, speaking about it aloud, sometimes smiling, more often frowning.

"Could I have a drink? If it's not too much trouble."

"No trouble."

Drury soaked his bandana in the seep-spring and squeezed the water into Royal's mouth. He had done it a dozen times for the dying man, who didn't remember.

He had shot and roasted a rabbit, but the effort of eating was beyond Royal.

"We've been here four days," he said.

Royal gulped the dribble of water and rolled his head to signify he'd had enough, couldn't swallow more. "It won't be much longer," he whispered.

Squatting on his heels by him, Drury made no comment. False encouragement was foolish to a man who knew he was done-for. He bit on the stem of an empty pipe that had belonged to the Texas cattle buyer, wishing he had tobacco, wishing for many unattainable things.

Presently he grew aware of Royal's eyes scanning his ravaged face. "Drury, you puzzle me," Royal whispered. "The more I know you, the more the mystery—"

"What's bothering you? I'll answer anything you ask. It'll do to pass the time," Drury said.

He immediately regretted using that phrase. It made him appear to be waiting for Royal to die, to be rid of the burden. He didn't mean that. He had grown to know Royal better, as Royal had come to know him. Not as lawman and outlaw. As two men together in a desperate fix.

"What bothers me is how and why a man of your stamp went renegade." Royal's eyes searched Drury's face. "Turning against your own people. Killing, looting, burning—in God's name, how could you do it? You—*you*—who've helped me to the end! How did it begin?"

Pondering, Drury let a moment go by. "The way you put it," he said somberly, "is how it would be put at my trial. No ifs or maybes. Any Tuscon jury would find me guilty. Any Tuscon judge would hang me!"

"Now, wait! A fair trial—"

"Fair trial, my foot!"

"Our judicial system," said Royal, rather pontifically, "is based on the belief that the accused is innocent until proved guilty."

"Balls!" said Drury. "I wouldn't stand the ghost of a chance. Give a dog a bad name, and you may as well hang it. That goes for justice in our territorial courts these days. Those fellows in Cometi, the Rangers, they treated me like I'd been already tried and found guilty!"

"Your reputation—"

"My evil reputation, yes. That's what I mean. On the strength of it, what court wouldn't convict me?" Rising to his feet, he stared down at Royal. "You, for instance. If you were on the jury, would you even listen to my defense?"

"I'd try to."

"But prejudice would block your ears! You don't doubt I'm guilty as charged—the full bill. Murder, torture, all the rest of it."

"I wish," Royal said, "that I could find reason to doubt your guilt. In fact—" he smiled faintly—"I'd like that. I'd be grateful for it."

"Grateful? Why?"

"I'm dying. In my last hours I'd like knowing that— that I'm cared for by a Christian man. Not by a savage. A white savage."

"How selfish man is," Drury nodded. "You, me, we're both selfish."

"That's a cynical remark," Royal observed. "Tell me —when you carried me here, were you only thinking about yourself?"

"You bet! I did it to be on top. To be superior. To set you down for that goddam cigarette!"

"That? No, no. Drury, you're lying to yourself. You didn't wear yourself out carrying me here for revenge. That's not the act of a bloody-handed renegade. Nor

33

this—taking care of me to the end." Royal stopped for breath. "Give your defense. I'll listen."

Drury paced the floor of the cave. "In Mexico," he said, "there's a small tribe of Indians living in a valley, about thirty miles south of Cometi. They're an offshoot branch of Apaches and they keep pretty much to themselves. They farm and trade for their living. Other Apaches scorn them because they're peaceful. They're called Bloodstoners," Drury went on. "Once a year they trek up here into Arizona Territory to a certain spot, secret to them, where they gather garnet stones. Bloodstones. Garnets are found on ant hills. The ants bring them to the surface and discard them. The Bloodstoner Apaches work them into jewelry—necklaces and the like—which they sell."

"You're straining my belief," Royal protested. "Red garnets are valuable. They're semiprecious gems. Hasn't it ever occurred to those Indians to dig down into the ant hills and get at the source, instead of only taking what the ants bring up?"

Drury grinned briefly. "That's the white man's way. Take it all at one swat. To the Indians it would be like chopping down the tree that provides fruit, or killing the goose that laid golden eggs. No, they give thanks for the little harvest and preserve its source for future years, future generations."

"You make them seem almost civilized."

"In their way, that little tribe has been civilized for a hell of a long time. Not as we understand it, no. But maybe they're ahead of us."

"That's incredible!"

"Is it? They realize the dangers of wealth—the dangers of owning more riches than their neighbors. Envy, greed, robbery. Great wealth, gold, caused utter ruin to the Aztec Nation. The Spanish plunderers

34

slaughtered them for it. If the Aztecs had been poor, they would have survived."

"You have a point," Royal granted.

"The Bloodstoners have a legend," Drury went on. "Ages ago, they say, a holy man came among them. A Black Robe, as the Indians called priests. He Christianized them, God knows how. He taught them all they know and persuaded them to settle down. I guess he was a monk attached to an expedition of Spanish explorers, *conquistadores* if you will. He got lost, or maybe he chose to stay and convert the savage heathens —to the glory of heaven and the salvation of his soul, which probably needed it."

"You're damned cynical."

"Yeah. Whatever became of that lonely monk, nobody will ever know."

"I wonder," Royal mused. "Those early Spanish friars kept written records. They were scribes. The old archives in Mexico City are said to be clogged with their reports."

"How would he have got his report to Mexico City?"

"God knows."

Painstakingly, the Jesuit padre had inscribed, "God knows in His infinite wisdom why I write this journal, for no hope exists that other eyes than mine will read it. The Apaches, ancient scourge of this barren land, do mock me with threats. Torture and death be my fate. The pitiless Apache nation spreads far beyond our province to extensions no one has knowledge of. It be so vast it exceeds kingdoms of Europe. Their number is countless. Their manner of living is savagely cruel, engaged constantly in war. Murder and robbery is their sport. They make horrid ravages everywhere. They are fierce beyond belief, and torture is their joy.

"Indeed it is a mercy of God that these Apaches are ignorant of their own strength. Were they united, there is no place which could be held against them. Yet it is feared they will do this. They are changing their methods of war. Formerly their attacks were timed to the full moon, the so-called Apache moon. Now they commit their hideous crimes by dark, slaying men and women and children of neighbor tribes, taking young females captive into slavery of the most vile . . .

"Comes now to me a leader of these detestable Apaches. A chief. Demands he that I must cure him of his disease. Else I die by slow fire. I do not possess medicines."

Later, the Jesuit padre inscribed in his journal, "Praise to God. I cured the chief. His disease was put upon him by a witch doctor, a sorcerer in the service of a rival chief. There are many such. These savage Apaches do fight among themselves and vie for power —like wicked children, untrustful and hateful. Placing secretly a small pebble in my mouth, I did suck at the sick chief's chest, then showed him the pebble, saying it had been the root of his disease and I had fetched forth the villain by the Power of My Most Almighty Father. May He forgive me. . . ."

Pages later, the padre wrote in his journal, "Grace of God. Twenty and seven Apaches have taken baptism. Now I lead them and the chief south to a goodly valley where with God's help they may live and prosper, tilling the soil, no more war. . . ."

Royal closed his dulling eyes wearily. "What have those Indians got to do with your case?" he asked. "The subject strikes me as, er—immaterial."

"I beg your patience," Drury said. "I first met them, the Bloodstoners, when they were gathering garnets. I'd been mustanging and prospecting for gold on the side. I took a fall and banged myself up, miles from my camp. Those Indians took care of me."

"That's not reason enough to turn renegade!"

Drury nodded agreement. "A team of railroad surveyors reached our camp. They had an Army escort and a hired guide, an Army scout named Soderman."

"Harl Soderman? I've heard of him. The famous scout."

"Yeah. That Indian-fighting hero." Drury's tone was dry. "Soderman opened fire at us right away. Our camp was by a spring, only water in miles, but we'd have shared it with anybody who asked. The soldiers fired, too. Squad of juniper recruits, under a bonehead corporal. Didn't know any better than follow Soderman's example. So we had a fight."

"You said the Bloodstone Apaches are peaceful."

"I didn't say they'll stand still to be killed! After all, they're Apaches. I sided them. They were my friends. Soderman took a bullet in his neck. My bullet. Two soldiers got killed. I helped my Indian friends to get back home. We were hunted all the way. A federal warrant was on me, so I stayed there with them in Mexico, in their valley. Worked with them. They paid me the honor of making me their bloodbrother. It's a real honor, believe me. A rare honor."

"But it made a renegade of you," Royal murmured.

"Not to my mind. If it had, I'd never have come back north alone," Drury countered.

"Why did you?"

"To bring warning of a planned uprising."

"How did you know of it in that valley, where you say your redskin friends are civilized Christians who shun the warpath?"

"Other Apaches visit there to trade for garnets, which

they believe are lucky stones. They brag about what they've done and what they'll do. This is their year. The Army's been letting its old soldiers go, and bringing in green replacements. My good Bloodstoner friends told me the Apaches bragged how they'd chop the Army to bits."

"So you came back, though you knew there's a federal warrant out for you."

"I hoped to reach Tucson with the warning, but I didn't get past Cometi. Those Arizona Rangers wouldn't listen. If they'd been looking for me, lying in wait for me there, I'd have got wind of it in time. But they weren't, and I didn't."

"And now," Royal said, "your warning is too late." He rolled his head on the ground, sighing. "The Apaches have begun their rampage, eh? How many?"

Drury spread his hands and let them fall. "Hell knows. All those from their *rancherias* below the border, for sure. And the Chiricahuas on this side. The Mescalleros and Jicarillos. And if the reservation Apaches join it—thousands."

"God! White people fighting for their lives, against hordes of savages! D'you think it's going on now?"

"Now or soon. I don't know." Drury stopped his pacing. He stood stock-still facing the open mouth of the cave, squinting against the brilliant sunshine outside. "Not yet, maybe. Many Apaches have heard of me. Probably the word's leaked out that I came north with the warning. It could cause them to delay their plans till they're sure I failed."

"You put a good deal of importance on yourself," Royal observed.

Drury nodded absently. "I see moving dots way out there. Only Apaches would willingly travel this country on foot. Guess they cut our sign somewhere along the

38

way. Lost it and now they're spread out, quartering to pick it up again."

Royal raised his head with an effort. "How much time have we got left, do you reckon?"

"I doubt they can track us here before dark."

Clasping his hands under his head, Royal composed himself on the floor of the cave. "I won't last that long," he muttered, without regret. "What they do to my body doesn't matter. Can't hurt me. When the soul departs— Drury, escape while you can."

Drury snorted a harsh laugh. "Escape where to? I'm posted by name and description, accused of taking part in practically every Apache raid for the past two years. If I escape the Apaches, white men will hang me! No, I'll keep you company."

"Change your name and description. Shave off that beard and cut your hair. Shed those buckskin rags. Get into some civilized clothes. There'd be no difference then to speak of between you and me." Royal paused, closing his eyes. "That's an idea for you. I won't need my clothes after I'm dead. Nor my name. Nothing."

"I don't rob the dead."

"No robbery. A gift. Listen to me. Listen close. My full name is Kenneth Claude Royal. My papers and badge are in my pocket. Take them."

"D'you actually mean I should try to—? You must be out of your head! It'd never work."

"It would. Tell you why." Royal sounded lucid, reasonable. "I was sent from Denver to pick up a prisoner in Tucson but when I got there he was dead. Hanged himself in his cell. So I got orders to go on down to Cometi and take you off the Rangers' hands, which I did."

"Yeah, but—"

"Dammit, don't you see? I'm not known by sight

here in your godforsaken Arizona. You could pass for me, with my papers. We're about the same size, same color of hair and eyes."

Drury watched the moving dots in the far distance, ants gradually inching nearer. "How about your family, your kin?"

"I don't have any family left and I'm not married," Royal answered. His voice had sunk, weakening to scarcely more than a whisper. "My next-of-kin, an uncle, is an Army officer, who's stationed permanently back East."

"You'd trust me with your name?"

"I give you leave to borrow it until you're out of the Territory. I owe it to you. Go far away to some place where nobody ever heard of Jim Drury. Oregon or somewhere. When you're safe, you might write to my uncle. Tell him—just tell him I died clean."

While Drury wondered at the phrase, Royal explained, "My father cut me off years ago, for good reason. He was an Army officer, too. I was a disgrace to him. Flunked West Point. Got into scrapes. Showed up drunk at my mother's funeral. That was the day he slammed the door on me." Royal fought for breath. "I've been cleaning my slate ever since that sorry day."

That accounted for Royal's severity, Drury mused. Once a scapegrace wildling, reformed he had bent to the other extreme and become austerely correct. But all the time, behind that inhuman surface, he was very human. The granite was thin and now it had cracked wide open.

Royal closed his eyes again. For a while, senses slipping, he mumbled unintelligibly, then the cave was quiet. In an hour, regaining consciousness when Drury tried giving him water, he pronounced clearly, "You should be on your way."

By the sharp-edged shadow at the mouth of the cave he could see that the day was waning. He looked up with a sort of humorous exasperation at the bearded, ravaged visage over him, accepting the fact of his helplessness, the control of a man who was in control of himself. The wakeful presence of Drury had watched over them both for days and nights. Renegade Drury.

"My friend—be on your way. There's no use—"

"There's time yet," Drury said.

Royal, his face thin and shallow with coming death, managed a ghastly smile. "Not for me—"

CHAPTER FIVE

Slogging along the bed of a dry arroyo, the squad of footsore infantrymen, carrying two wounded, straggled to a halt. They were green soldiers, thirsty, hungry, glumly mutinous over the absence of regular rations. Discipline was a thing of the past. Parade-ground drill, useless relic of olden days when armies had marched full-front into battle, was sloughed off.

It was a derelict detachment, homeless, no post for it to return to. The post had been wiped out.

The noncom, a stout corporal who chested a row of faded ribbons, barked belatedly, "Squa-a-ad, halt!" They were already halted, sinking to rest in the sandy bed of the arroyo, on their knees, some on their backs. Remembering way back when he had been a juniper, the corporal couldn't blame them. It took time to make a tough soldier.

He had held them together. At gunpoint he had stopped some from going off on their own hook. He was scouring around, picking up stray soldiers from the defeated garrisons. Disaster wasn't new to him, he having fought in the Civil War, and personal misfortune had engraved dour lines on his rugged face.

He stared at the small party that emerged from the next bend ahead of the arroyo—three soldiers carrying a fourth, bloodily hurt, preceded by a tall civilian who stalked forefront as if in command of them.

The corporal, though he didn't actually dislike civilians, believed that civilians took second-place to the Army, especially in time of war. It grated him to see one leading the three soldiers, whom he recognized as belonging to his outfit, the green Tres Santos garrison, now broken and scattered. So he snapped roughly, "Who're you?" while he off-shouldered his rifle.

One of the three soldiers snapped back, "Ease it, old two-stripe! He pulled us out of a jackpot. He pistoled the Injuns who got us pinned down. His name's Ken."

The corporal nodded to the tall civilian. "Howdy, Mr. Ken. My name's Lagerfeld." He paused, studying the man and watching touchily for his reaction. "Corporal Jacob Lagerfeld. My friends call me Jake."

His friends were enlisted men and battered old soldiers who liked and respected him. Not the swank officers, the West Point 100 per cent true American elite that could detect at a syllable a New York Jew. Many times he had been passed over for promotion, despite efficiency and hard-earned medals. Those goddam officers.

Jim Drury extended his right hand. "Glad to meet you, Corporal. Hope some day I can call you Jake."

Corporal Lagerfeld shook hands, warily, asking, "Where do you fit in? The Tres Santos got jumped—scattered to hell! By the reservation Apaches. Took us by surprise. The only civvies we've seen since were dead! How come you're alive?"

"I know this country," Drury answered him, "and I know the ways of Apaches—far better than you do, probably."

"Prob'ly, yeah. This lousy Arizona! Ev'rything here stings, pricks, bites—"

"You're lost. If you keep on down this arroyo, you'll walk into a pack of Apaches."

"Kee-rist! Are the red bastards ev'rywhere?"

"Everywhere there are whites to slaughter. Particularly, most particularly, soldiers. All respect to you, Corporal, but you better let me guide you."

43

"Give him command!" urged the speaking soldier of the trio and the others grunted assent. "He knows what he's doing, which is more'n you do, two-stripe!" A barracks lawyer, that one. There was always one such in every company; always right, hated by the noncoms who considered themselves lords of law.

Corporal Lagerfeld shrugged. Aware then that his shoulders sagged, he braced up and announced sternly, "Mr. Ken is our guide. Take your orders from him."

"No," Drury said. "I can only offer advice. You give the orders, Corporal Lagerfeld."

"As you wish, sir."

"Wish, sir, my ass! Let's get this mob out o' here before we're clobbered to hell, Jake! The Apaches are coming up on all sides. Get moving!"

"Okay, Ken. Squa-a-ad, over the bank, double-quick!"

They vacated the arroyo only a minute before the Apache onrush and made a running fight during which one of the wounded died and had to be left behind. No time for burial. Every man was on his gun, firing for life.

A red-striped warrior sprang up and dashed at Lagerfeld in mad fury, gibbering curses, swinging aloft a fearsome weapon fashioned from a knife bound crosswise to a club. An Apache tomahawk for hacking or throwing. The warrior was elderly, impatient of firearms and had reverted to a weapon he liked best.

Lagerfeld and Drury both shot him down. The tomahawk spun end-over-end from the warrior's throw. Dodging it, Lagerfeld grunted, "Crazy, that duck!"

"He was an old chieftain," Drury said, somberly scanning the body, the red paint, the short pigtail braided with strips of red flannel. "He had to live up to his old reputation."

"You sound like you knew him."

"I met him once. They'll be drawing back now, Jake."

"Damned if they ain't. Look there. Was it killing the old chief did it?"

"Partly. They want his body. It's a matter of—well, call it honor. So they're inviting us to pull out and leave it for 'em. He was a big man. Earned his funeral."

The corporal whooshed a breath. "They're welcome to it!"

Evening, the squad lay in a foothill valley, no fire allowed, no smoking. Exhausted, the men twitched and muttered in their sleep. Those posted on outguard had to be relieved every hour, or they dozed off. The wakeful wounded stared up at the darkening sky, afraid of their bleak prospects. All around, the approaching night whispered of peril.

Lagerfeld, returning from making his round of the outguards, stretched himself out on the ground beside Drury. "These doughfoots!" he commented. "They ain't got stamina. Know what I mean? Stamina. The good ol' guts like we had, their age."

"They're doing okay," Drury said, knowing better than to downgrade any man's outfit even if he asked for it. "I don't hear any whimpers."

"Nor you won't," Lagerfeld averred, reversing tack. "They took a mauling at Tres Santos. Tres Santos— that means three Saints, don't it? What three?"

"Couldn't say."

"You don't talk much. Me, I like talking. With certain folks, that is."

"Takes all kinds, Jake."

"Ain't it a fact."

45

Searching for a subject for conversation to feed the corporal's talkative mood, Drury inquired, "What became of the officers at Tres Santos?"

"Dead. The hostiles attacked officers' quarters first and torched the row. After midnight. Our commanding officer, now very deceased and unlamented at least by me," Lagerfeld related elaborately, "rushed out in his nightshirt, bellering like a bull. At rough count I'd say he stopped fourteen bullets. It couldn'ta happened to a better bastard than him."

"D'you hate all officers?"

"No. Only his kind, the kind that treats men under him like dirt. Well, his time was up anyway. A new man's coming to take command of the post. Or was. Ain't no post left there now to take command of, just ashes. Be a surprise for that new C.O. if he ever got there."

"A slim if!"

Shrugging, Lagerfeld bit off a chew of hard-twist tobacco. "That's his worry. We've got ours. Any idea where we are?"

"We're in the Palo Verde foothills," Drury said.

"That don't mean much to me."

"It means mountain passes ahead, east. The Palo Verdes stretch thirty miles or more north-and-south, and we can't turn back and keep our hair."

"So we can cross the goddam mountains, eh?"

"Tonight. Unless you'd sooner make a stand here in daylight tomorrow, when the Apaches surround us. Jake, you're wobbly for sleep. We all are. But we didn't come this far to give up the ghost, did we?"

Lagerfeld rolled over on the ground and tiredly sat up, dabbing his bloodshot eyes with tobacco spittle to keep them smartingly open. "Okay, Ken. You're the guide." He offered his precious stub of rope tobacco. "Chew?"

Next day in the higher, rougher country, they picked up six more stray infantrymen: four from the Tres Santos catastrophe, wandering far from the wiped-out post and two survivors of a San Carlos patrol that had been chopped to pieces.

"I dunno this goddam country," Lagerfeld said to Drury, slogging alongside him. "I'm new here." He stumbled, caught his balance, and swayed. "I'm done. You take command o' this mob."

Drury wrapped an arm around him. "You don't give up that easy. Not you, Jake."

The afternoon of that day, clambering through a mountain pass, breath short because of high altitude, they met head-on a platoon that was marching westward. Amazingly, the platoon was equipped with a mule team-drawn baggage wagon and an ambulance—a spindly wheeled vehicle, canvas-covered, drawn by mules like the heavier baggage wagon.

The platoon sergeant in the lead snappily gave the order to halt. He swept a stare over the bunch of bedraggled fugitives. Seeing no officer with them, nor any noncom who outranked him, he demanded. "What mob are you? Where you from?"

It was the tone, more than the words of common and casual Army greeting, that grated. Lagerfeld straightened up. Drury could feel his bristling wrath.

"This is a mob o' fighting sons-o'-bitches from hell!" Lagerfeld snarled back, and the doughfoot greeners behind him brisked up at the rare compliment. "Who the goddam are *you*?"

The sergeant blinked. More mildly, realizing that he was confronting battle-scarred troops, half-mad, he said, "We're the major's escort. The major was due to take command of the Tres Santos garrison, but we got sidetracked."

"By Apaches?"

"Yeah. We've been under fire. The major got damaged a bit. Bullet in his leg."

"Welcome to the flock!" said Drury. "Turn back east with us. We've got Apaches on our tails."

"So've we," the sergeant said.

"East?"

"East, west. North, south. They're everywhere. Mister, who're you?" The sergeant's eyes glinted distrust. There were always the evil whites, gun-runners, rum-peddlers.

"I'm a trapper and mustanger and a gold prospector on the side. My name's Ken." He was reluctant to borrow the full name. The soldiers with him had accepted his self-introduction. Surname, given name, or adopted, it made no difference to them, so many having enlisted under false names for personal and private reasons.

"Ken's the best scout I ever knew!" declared Lagerfeld.

Something kept the sergeant's suspicion rampant. Perhaps it was Drury's face and build, teasing an uncertain memory of a description printed on a government-issued wanted bill. Or he sensed a concealed wariness. "Scout? He just now said he's a trapper and mustanger. Have you seen any proof of who he is?"

"Sure! He got us through the Apaches. That's proof. He don't need nobody to vouch for him. He can smell them bastards a mile off, and he's a fighting—"

"Watch your cussing!"

Lagerfeld eyed the sergeant in open-mouthed astonishment. Army blackmouth was simply an adjunct to speech, accepted among soldiers. "Goddam it, why should I?" A soldier with any length of service could hardly string three words together without an oath. The commonest objects acquired profane or bawdy slang-terms. The habit made for difficulty whenever talking to civilians, especially females.

The sergeant turned and pointed toward the ambulance. "There's why."

"Your damaged major?" Corporal Lagerfeld queried, scant in respect. "Creest, ain't he heard Army talk before? Is he a f— preacher, or something?"

"No. He's regular Army. But his daughter's in there with him. She's a lady."

"Creest! Ken—"

"Yeah, I know. A woman—here!" To the sergeant, Drury said, "I want to see the major."

"You're a civilian." The distrust remained.

"A citizen. For your information, Sergeant, citizens' taxes support the Army which only exists on our say-so. What's your name?"

"O'Trist."

"Sergeant O'Trist, take me to your commanding officer, the major, please."

Hesitating, Sergeant O'Trist compromised by splaying his hand to his holstered pistol. "March ahead of me!"

"I'm not drilled to the quick-step, Sergeant O'Trist, so I'll take my own gait." Drury's gait was long-striding, trained soundless, ever vigilant to avoid dried twigs and smooth pebbles.

At the ambulance, Sergeant O'Trist called, "Major, sir! Here's a civilian wants to see you."

"Ask him to come in," replied a voice inside.

"Major, sir, we've met a mob of stragglers from the west. They say they're chased. This civilian's with 'em." The sergeant's tone of voice conveyed that he didn't trust the civilian. "He's armed."

"Ask him," repeated the voice, "to come in." Then, "Don't worry, Sergeant—" placatingly—"I'm armed, and so are you, aren't you?"

"Yes sir."

"Very well, then."

The preliminaries exasperated Drury, who cut in, "Major, I want a word with you. It's urgent. Let's not waste time."

There was a short silence, as if the officer was weighing the impatient words. "Come in. Linley, open up for the gentleman."

A flap of the canvas front-curtain drew open. Drury glimpsed a feminine arm and shoulder, part of a face, and one eye that peered fleetingly down at him. He stepped up onto the wheel-hub and, bending at the waist, ducked into the ambulance.

Sergeant O'Trist rattled off the names of half-dozen privates and cracked an order. "Stand by on the sharp!" And he didn't mean for Apaches.

CHAPTER SIX

The afternoon sunlight, shaded off by the west wall of the mountain pass, did not strike the ambulance's canvas top. The brightness of the clear sky directly above only gave the canvas a weak glow that was shadowless inside the ambulance.

Drury paused to adjust his eyes. In a moment he was aware of two bunks, one empty. On the other bunk a man reclined, fully dressed except for his right leg which, laid bare, was bandaged below the knee.

"How d'you do," the man said in a tone of formal politeness. "Excuse me for not rising," he added, and that tone was dry.

His thick thatch of hair was stark white. On his face were engraved lines half-humorous and half-cynical. He seemed both fatherly and disillusioned. An officer who, sitting in judgment on week-end drunks, would probably temper justice with mercy, knowing that mercy went wasted in most cases. Yet he exuded a youthful vigor, like many veterans.

A young woman stood motionless at the head of the empty bunk. Drury paid her a long glance, noting the pistol that she held in both hands, a heavy .44 Peacemaker pointed at him. She wasn't beautiful, at least not in the style of dance-hall girls he had known. Her hair was drawn back in a knot, which exposed clearly the ivory-pale face, a cameo carved in—he could think of no better word—ivory.

He judged her to be in the mid-twenties, maybe twenty-four. An old maid, loveless, devoted to her father. God in heaven, what a waste of womanhood! With men in this godforsaken land, virile men, hungering to shower love on a woman and to beget children—

"How d'you do, Major," Drury responded levelly. In his best voice he said to the young woman, "I'd take it as a kindly courtesty, ma'am, if you'd lower that gun off me. It might go off. Your finger, ma'am, is on the trigger."

"My daughter," said the major, "is not a ma'am. She's unmarried."

"More's the pity. It should be remedied." Drury cast a bold look at the young woman, for the hell of it. To his utter amazement, the ivory-cameo blushed warm red. The blush made her very young, much younger than he had judged. Twenty? Nineteen? His male senses quickened. She was wholly desirable.

"Linley, put down that gun," the major told his daughter. "I think we have a gentleman here."

Drury had been often angered by Easterners who took for granted that Westerners were uncouth illiterates. They based their presumptions upon fallacies created by hack scribblers and bogus adventurers. Drury wasn't the only trapper who carried books in his pack.

A popular coffee brand gave away cheaply printed copies of classics. Drury had heard them read aloud in bunkhouses and roundup camps, where pro-and-con criticism was apt to grow hot and pungently profane. They largely were responsible for occasional flights of language, sardonically elaborate, of cowhands when in argument—which astonished no end any Easterner within earshot.

But the image had been set, made concrete by penny-a-line newspaper scribes for their Eastern readers. Westerners were illiterate. Indians were savages. Any departure from the image was ignored. Never mention men of education who happened to be living in the west. Nor mention that old Washakie, chief of Shoshonies, studied the writings of Emerson. Don't crack the image of white barbarian and red savage, for fear of decreased sale of newspapers.

"I heard my sergeant talk to you," the major remarked. "You didn't tell him who you are. I ask you now—I demand to know, rather—who *are* you?"

Here it was. Drury saw no way out of it. Proof of his identity. Papers. "I'm a U.S. special marshal."

"Your credentials, please."

He produced slowly the badge, the identity papers that belonged to another man, Kenneth Claude Royal, dead in a cave. "I'm Ken Royal," he said. "Kenneth Claude Royal." The lie came so easily then, that instantly on the speaking of it he became and *was* Ken Royal, blacksheep of a moderately distinguished family. For Drury had been his family's blacksheep—a drifter from conventional family paths. He had rebelled and gone his own way at an early age, sometimes regretting it in times of desperate adversity but never calling back for help.

The girl, at the head of the empty bunk, uttered a small gasp. Drury looked at her, seeing the gun hanging slack in her hands. Then the major said, "So you're Ken! I haven't seen you since you were a boy. In Concord, New Hampshire. Don't s'pose you remember."

"No, sir."

"It was only ten minutes. You were in that military academy. My brother, your father, wouldn't take you with us to New York. I cussed him out afterwards for it." Tardily, full realization burst upon the major. "Holy bejeesus! Linley, he's Ken! Your cousin!"

He paid no further regard to the identity papers,

handing them back. "It's fantastic, meeting like this. I'm Eric Royal, your uncle!"

The shock of it hit Drury. He could only say numbly "It can't be! No, no! You were stationed permanently East." He remembered Royal telling him.

Major Eric Royal grimaced. "Nothing is permanent in the Army, except inside politics. There was a shake-up. I drew field duty. A tour of duty as commander of the Tres Santos post. At Tucson I was given an escort from Camp Lowell—"

"Tres Santos is wiped out."

"Right! We've been under fire. From hostiles. We're trying to get back to Tucson." The major extended his right hand. "Glad to meet you again, Ken. You've grown tall, like all us Royals. No mistaking you for a Royal."

They gripped hands firmly.

"The Royals are Virginia people, as you know," Major Royal went on, rather boring Drury who didn't give much of a damn where any family came from. "They were originally from Cornwall. Cornishmen. South England."

"Yeah. Major—"

"Call me Uncle Eric. I *am* your uncle."

"It's strange to me," Drury said. "I'll call you Major, if you don't mind. I haven't had any family in years." He bowed his head to the girl. "I'm happy to know you, Cousin Linley—most happy. We've never met before, have we?"

He was seeking for knowledge to sustain his part, having committed himself irrevocably to the identity of U.S. Deputy Marshal Kenneth Claude Royal. Inwardly, he damned Royal for having talked him into this. Royal had meant well but he hadn't made allowances for tricks of fate such as this.

"We've met. At your mother's funeral. I was a little girl. You didn't notice me. You were—you were—"

"Drunk!"

She nodded. "Even I could see that. It was disgusting."

"I've changed."

"Yes. Indeed you have, Cousin Ken."

Was there irony in her voice: a tinge of disbelief? Drury wasn't sure. She might have detected a discrepancy. Kids were so observant. A freckle or mole might have stuck in her memory.

"Thank you, Cousin Linley. May I ask why you're here?"

Major Royal answered for her: "Linley kept house for me back East. After I got my transfer orders, nothing was left for her there. No relatives she could go to. It seemed best for her to accompany me out here. The living accommodations at Tres Santos were adequate, I was told. A quiet post. Small garrison."

With, Drury thought to himself, eligible young officers eager to pay court to an unattached young woman. Coffee and cake on the verandah, dances in the mess hall, strolls by moonlight. A quiet and fairly comfortable little post, safely located on a tame reservation where the curious habits of Indians provided only a source of entertainment and conversation.

The major hadn't bargained on Apaches. They weren't tamed yet, not by a long shot. They regarded this vast land as their province, to roam at will, and hated the intruders who crowded them, forcing them back or pocketing them on reservations. The pressure had constantly increased: Wrongheaded orders from far-off officials. Contempt from junior field officers and enlisted men. Cheating from traders.

Now the Apaches' thin patience had waned and

waves of murder swept over the land. Whites had scant tolerance for Apaches and Apaches had none at all for whites.

"If you don't mind a suggestion," Drury said, "this is a good place for a rest. Gives us cover. Up on the banks, pickets can keep lookout in all directions. The soldiers with me are about done in."

"How good a scout are you, Ken?"

"I know the country, and I've had some acquaintance with the ways of Apaches," Drury allowed cautiously.

"We need you badly, then. You *have* changed in the years since last I saw you. Sergeant!"

Sergeant O'Trist poked his head into the ambulance. "Sir?"

"We'll rest here. But no fires, no smoking. Put pickets up the banks, and be sure they stay awake and sharp-eyed. Break out some cold rations from the baggage wagon. And water."

"You mean for everybody, sir? We're awful short. None to spare." The sergeant cut an inhospitable glance at Drury, who had seated himself on the empty cot. "That feller—"

"This gentleman," interrupted the major with mild emphasis, "is now our scout and guide. He has the knowledge and experience we lack."

"I hope we can trust him, sir."

"No question of that. For one thing, he is a United States deputy marshal."

The sergeant's big face displayed complete disbelief. "He's said he's a trapper, mustanger, gold prospector and scout! Now he claims to be a federal lawman! What next? Beg your pardon sir, but he don't ring true to me."

"He does to me. He happens to be my nephew."

It was too much for the sergeant. His face crimsoned.

He stared rigidly at nothing, as if dealt a stunning blow, then withdrew his head from the ambulance, repeating in a choked mumble, "Beg your pardon, sir—"

Drury thought: I'll have trouble from him if I'm not careful, very careful. He's got a sharp instinct, like mine but in a different way. He senses I'm false. So does the girl.

Major Royal chuckled softly. "Sergeant O'Trist had that coming to him! First time I've seen him flustered since we left Tucson."

"You led him into it," said his daughter, unsmiling. "It was unfair to him."

"He deserved it, Linley, for his attitude toward Ken, your cousin."

"Until you told him, he didn't know—"

"He knows now." The major turned back to Drury. "Linley has adopted the sergeant. Or the sergeant has adopted Linley. They're thick as thieves. His Irish crust hides a sentimental streak."

"A corporal has sort of adopted me," Drury said. "Corporal Jacob Lagerfeld. Not Irish, nor sentimental. A good man." It earned him a level stare from the girl. "Jake," he said, "took it on himself to gather up strays from Tres Santos. Junipers. He's shaped 'em into bearcats."

"Sergeant O'Trist could do the same!" Linley retored in defense of her friend.

"That takes a real soldier."

The emphasis rested lightly on the word *real*, which brought a combative sparkle to her eyes. She opened her lips to voice another retort. But then she perceived his faint grin and realized that he was baiting her, leading her on, as her father had led Sergeant O'Trist into a pit of embarrassment. She colored furiously and was silent.

Major Royal heaved himself up to a sitting posture on his cot, legs over the side. He tugged the creases from his blue tunic and wiped back his white hair. "I want to meet him, that excellent corporal! Call him in, Ken, will you?"

But at that moment a rifle cracked off and somebody yelled urgently, "Hostiles! Christ, they're all around us!"

CHAPTER SEVEN

The major, carried in the closed ambulance, hadn't had time to inspect the terrain. Hadn't taken the time. As officer in command, wounded or not, that should have been his first duty. He had no junior officers to shoulder the responsibility. Having behind him too many years of humdrum barracks life he had forgotten the essentials of wartime soldiering.

"How do we stand?" he rapped at Drury. And Linley's eyes conveyed to Drury a mute accusation: *You said this was a good place to rest!*

"Our position," Drury responded, "is strongly defensive if we make the most of it. We need more men up on the banks, fast, before the Apaches can get there and fire down on us."

"Tell O'Trist it's an order from me!"

"Sure—"

O'Trist bedamned. He found Corporal Lagerfeld pulling his boots back on, wincing and grunting curses, and he said to him swiftly, "Better split our bunch and man the banks, Jake! You take the right bank, I'll take the left."

"How 'bout letting the fat Irisher handle it? He's got a platoon."

"I don't know him. I do know you. We're boxed in."

Lagerfeld rose on sore feet, sighing morosely. "How many of 'em this time?" He put the question as if sure of its answer from Drury—Ken—infallible scout.

"Probably a hundred, thereabouts. We can't let 'em take the banks. They'd slaughter us. Like shooting fish in a barrel."

"See what you mean. Okay, Ken, we'll sling 'em off. Hey, men—!" It sounded like *Amen*.

Over a campfire one night, in deep thought, Drury had reached the conclusion that all men, including himself, were dangerous. The least of men, backed to the wall, becomes bearcat. That last, lonely place that you enter—the fear faced, death confronted—holds no further terror. You are then deadly, a fierce opponent. Any man who stepped beyond fear lost touch with humanity. He was a savage.

Up on the left bank—the west bank—the skittering shapes of Apache warriors were slithering onward through the chapparal that surrounded the pass. The lowering sun flicked on their naked backs, their greased black hair tied back in rag-bands.

"Don't fire yet," he muttered. "Pass the word. Heads down. Wait!"

He could hear the sibilant whispers of the foremost Apaches. He knew that the men with him held forefingers itchily tensed on triggers, nerves stretched cruelly taut. He hoped that Lagerfeld on the right bank would hold his men in control.

"Let 'em come up close! Then we fire heavy!"

This had to be figured to the instant, to shatter the creeping advance, smash the Apaches' self-confidence. Heaven guide Lagerfeld—he was under the same strain on the other bank. Drury watched the oncoming ripple in the brush. The Apaches didn't yet realize that they had been seen. They believed themselves to be so crafty. With good reason. They were.

"Ready to fire," Drury murmured to the man who crouched beside him. "Pass the word. I'll fire first, for the signal."

To shoot too soon, wasting the short supply of shells, would be as fatal as delaying too long. But how could he expect these bolo soldiers—junipers, some of them city youths—hardly knowing the workings of a firearm —to know that?

"Is it so, sir, that the harder you jerk the trigger the faster the bullet goes?"

He confirmed the youngster's whispered question with a nod.

The man who crouched beside him on his other side Drury discovered, was Sergeant O'Trist. The sergeant asked, "Don't you reckon they're close enough now?"

"Are you taking charge, Sergeant?"

"No. The major ain't my uncle! I just wish you'd shoot."

"Shoot with me. Now!"

Their rifles blared together, snicked on the reload, and then the line of rifles along the lip of the bank blasted a volley. On the instant, Lagerfeld on the east bank cracked an order—"Fire at will, men!"—that brought his men to triggering.

The blast of gunfire ripped holes in the attack. The creeping, darting shapes retreated, some cursing in what sounded like English—which could have been, these Apaches having lived around reservation garrisons and taken on a smatter of soldier blackmouth. Soldiers together could hardly converse without casual profanity. The Indians picked up the repeated words, most of the words pungent, four-letter and simple to pronounce.

Astoundingly, an Apache brave sprang up from the brush and charged forward, crying out, *"O, ha le! Awbizhayhe!"* He made straight for Sergeant O'Trist. He swung aloft a keen-edged machete.

"Tsago degi naleya—!"

A death chant. The buck was wounded, but sought glory in bloodshed and death, his heavy blade poised strong: a Mexican machete, sharp as razor. He wasn't failing in strength, this charging warrior.

Drury, his rifle emptied and no time to reload, knowing that Sergeant O'Trist was in the same fix, jumped up and slammed the warrior, first with rifle-butt and then with fist. The warrior collapsed, his machete circling end-over-end until it fell into the brush and was lost there.

"Thanks," said Sergeant O'Trist, very briefly, making it plain that he didn't relish saying it. "What was that redskin hooting about? He acted crazy."

"Singing his death chant. They don't do that till they're ready to die fighting. Maybe he was steamed up on trade rum. Maybe they all are, way they fight. It makes 'em reckless."

"We could use some o' that!"

"Speak for yourself, Sergeant. I don't need booze to fight on. I only like it when I'm relaxing afterward."

O'Trist scowled, reloading his rifle, scraping with his thumbnail the clogging wax residue from the breech so that the hammer would slam down unfouled. "You ain't Irish." Drink was his one weakness, though he regarded the imbibing of it as a strength.

"I'm Irish on my father's side," said Drury unthinkingly.

"With that name—Royal? That's a Limey name!"

"Ah, shut up! Here they come again!"

The sergeant grinned, aware that he had punched a hole in Royal's front. He didn't believe the man was genuine—despite the major's vouching for him and despite his killing of the onrushing Apache warrior. Royal just didn't ring true—

Sporadic attacks continued into nightfall, costing precious supplies of dwindling ammunition. At deep dark, two hours before moonrise, the Apaches at last fell back. Their campfires in the near distance glowed, then dimmed, surrounding the pass on all sides. They were either sleeping or preparing a mass assault. Unlike most, these Apaches had no particular fear of darkness.

The soldiers on the banks lay exhausted, muscles twitching, eyes smarting and skin tingling from the backfire flash of exploded cartridges. Some bowed their heads into their folded arms, uncaring what happened next, unable to care about themselves anymore.

"Junipers!" O'Trist snorted. "They ain't got the stuff! In my day—"

Old soldier. One of the intolerant. Bragging of past glories, deeds of superhuman valor, stamina, more imagined than real. Everlastingly comparing today's young crop with yesterday's heroes.

The contemptuous insult riled Drury. The young men of past years had possessed no more courage than did today's young men. Nor better stamina. He had been in action for desperate days and nights with Lagerfeld's bloody but unbowed group.

So he rasped, "These are the best soldiers you ever served with, goddam you! They've got guts! They don't lay back under fire, like your Camp Lowell coffee-coolers down there in the pass!"

That set the sergeant aback. His eyes glimmered appraisingly, O'Trist respected any man who stood up for his outfit. A noncom could break his heart over his bungling squad, but derogatory criticism from outsiders invited a punch in the jaw.

Before the sergeant could think of a reply, Drury continued, "How 'bout bringing your petted platoon up to relieve my men? Or does that require the major's permission—or an act of Congress—or special dispensation from Rome?"

"*Your* men?"

"Yes, mine! By charge of Corporal Lagerfeld—a goddam good soldier you could take lessons from!"

"Creest!" muttered the sergeant, shaken for once. "Ain't you a prickly fighty bastard!"

"I'm a fighter, but my birth was legitimate. My mother was a married lady. Be a little more careful what you call me."

"I'll bear that in mind."

"Please do," Drury said evenly.

Major Royal, hobbling on a stick, rapped a command to his platoon escort, which had remained guarding the baggage wagon and ambulance. "Get up there and relieve those men!" He had heard the angry flare-up between Drury and O'Trist, or parts of it when their raised voices crackled. "Double-quick!" he added, not wanting those two to get into a slugging brawl.

They came down the bank together, Drury and O'Trist, carefully avoiding contact. In the pass, men were stretched out on the bare ground. Corporal Lagerfeld and his men were straggling down the right bank and joined them for a rest.

"Sorry if I sounded off too hot," Drury said sparely.

The response was a grunt. Drury judged that a few words of apology couldn't mend the sergeant's ill will. To hell with him, then. They trudged to Major Royal, standing by the ambulance.

"Sir, the hostiles have withdrew," the sergeant reported. "No telling for how long, though. We did 'em damage, but they're a big bunch, tough."

"What are our casualties, Ken?" the major asked.

Despite barracks years of routine spit-and-polish, on the field of action he showed a leaning toward informality.

"None that I know of, Major. I haven't checked yet with Corporal Lagerfeld. He's—"

"We took advantage of natural cover, sir," O'Trist cut in, jealously asserting his rank. "They couldn't get real close at us. 'Cept one."

"Corporal?" The major summoned Lagerfeld.

He dragged to his feet, saluting raggedly. "I lost three men, sir. Killed. The cover's not so good up on the right bank. It looked like they'd take us if they kept on."

"Let me shake your hand, Corporal Lagerfeld. A job well done."

Sergeant O'Trist's face registered unhappy disapproval. His tradition expected officers to maintain correct military form, never allowing a moment's laxness in the presence of enlisted men.

Major Royal turned back to Drury. "Was that attack a feeler, do you think, to determine our strength? The corporal thinks they could have broken through if they had tried longer." He glanced around at the ambulance behind him, as his daughter emerged from it.

Drury shook his head. "They already knew our strength, after hounding you here from the east and us from the west. They joined forces, like us, except they spread a ring and we're packed in the middle."

"It don't take any bright brain to figure that!" O'Trist muttered.

"Apaches can scamper over these mountains faster than we can travel a trail, and a lot quieter," Drury continued. "So their natural tactics would be to keep on hitting us, at the least cost to themselves, wearing us down for their final attack. No reason for them to quit. They outnumber us. They're well armed. It takes an

Apache forever to get tired." He was arguing with the feeling that had risen in him, the keen sense, the alert animal instinct. "And yet—"

It had never misled him before. Why should it do so now? The silent alarm, within him, invariably clanged louder in proportion to the nearness of danger. The alarm subsided when the danger passed. It had subsided in him now.

"And yet?" Major Royal prompted him.

"I think," he answered slowly, "the Apaches have not only quit, they've pulled out." He grew conscious of Linley gazing at him strangely. His eyes had blanked over, masked and withdrawn for that moment while he probed inwardly his instinct. The girl was perceptive, acutely sensitive to moods around her.

"Incredible!" the major exclaimed. "It's contrary to all reason, as you've pointed out yourself! Sergeant, what do you say?"

"I say he's dead wrong, sir. You can see their fires from up on the bank, all around us. The devils are only resting for their next attack."

"Corporal?"

"I'd bet Ken's right, sir. Maybe the fires are just a blind to hold us here."

"They are, Jake," Drury said. "The Apaches have slipped off, God knows why. I don't know what to make of it," he admitted. "It's as though they got a sudden order to hurry off somewhere else. Like Army troops. But Apaches don't usually take orders from anybody. The closest they come to it is to agree to follow the directions of somebody who knows the set-up better than they do. A temporary arrangement, like me being your scout for the time being."

The major looked at him thoughtfully. "It's possible, then, that this whole uprising is being directed by someone who, as you put it, knows the set-up. Someone with intelligence and organizing ability. Central direction. That would indicate a white man, I should think, rather than a redskin."

There it was again, the downgrading of Indian intelligence, the underestimation of Indian ability. Still, the major's conclusion was sound enough, although it had been arrived at by unsound reasoning. There were Apache warchiefs who were capable of directing the uprising but to elect a supreme leader from one of the several tribes, without arousing mutiny among the others, would be difficult if not impossible. Therefore, if a supreme leader existed whose instructions went unchallenged, he was most likely not an Apache.

"We've all heard of that renegade—Jim Drury, known as White Apache," the major pursued. "He could be the man, eh? He's reputed to be intelligent. How I'd like to lay a gun on the infamous devil!"

Cold mice-feet scurried up and down Drury's spine. His scalp prickled. He changed the subject. "I'll go out and see if my hunch is correct."

"Out there? You'll do no such damned thing!"

"The hell I don't!"

"Ken, it's taking your life in your hands! I forbid it! That's an order!"

Drury quirked an eyebrow. "Major, let's get this squared up once and for all. Granted you're in command here. But I'm not an Army man. I hold onto my right to do what I think is best."

Corporal Lagerfeld, sighing, looked down at his feet. "Want me along, Ken?"

O'Trist, not to be outshone even at the risk of death, said, "No, I'll go with him."

"I'll go alone," Drury decided. "This is just a quick

looksee." Then to the major, "I'll be back before moonlight."

Watching the tall figure recede into the darkness down the pass, Major Royal spoke aloud his misgivings. "How can he be so sure of himself? On nothing more than a hunch!"

Lagerfeld shrugged, his confidence in Drury unswerving. "He goes on hunches. He can smell the enemy miles away. Sharpest scout I ever heard of. Seen him work."

Sergeant O'Trist snorted skeptically. The source of his distrust was too vague to pinpoint but it itched his mind. "Bet my boots that's the last we see of him!"

"I'll take that bet," said Lagerfeld. "Hope your boots fit me. Mine are about gone."

"Quiet!" the major rapped. "Quiet, all! Listen!"

The worn-out soldiers lay listening. Linley listened, her ears straining to catch the slightest sound of the tall man who had gone out alone. Nothing disturbed the silence of the pass, not even the wind.

CHAPTER EIGHT

On his return, walking upright and openly into the pass, Drury announced, "They're gone. Every man-jack of 'em."

"You're certain?" Major Royal asked.

"I paid a visit to every fire. None's tended to." Drury pulled off his shirt and shook it. "Lice! In my pants, too. Linley, turn your back, I'm stripping off." He shed his pants, grumbling, "A soap bath and scrub for me, we ever reach water."

The reclining soldiers grinned in commiseration, those who were awake. All of them were affected to some degree by the voraciously blood-sucking lice and fleas that fondly fastened upon unwashed bodies.

Clothing himself, Drury said, "I still don't understand it, why they left. We better move before they come back. This spot's okay for a stand. A short stand. No good for a siege, though. Before long we'd be out of water, grub, ammo. Agree, Major?"

"Agree. Your hunch proved right, Ken. From now on I won't argue. Where do we move to?"

"East. Starting now."

"East is the way we came, my platoon. It was alive with hostile Apaches."

"Did you say you wouldn't argue?"

"Pardon!" The major inclined his head. "East it shall be."

"Then north, soon as we clear these mountains," Drury said. He laid out the terrain in his mind's eye, examining it, all its features and distances. "Our best bet—our only bet—is Camp Lowell at Tucson. Where you started out from."

"I confess I don't know the way back there from here. So much of this godawful country looks the same. Sand, cactus, dry creekbeds—"

"You've got me to guide you back to Tucson."

"Yes, of course. Tucson. I didn't have time to see much of it last time around." The major wasn't too old to regret lost opportunities. Those music-filled cantinas; those luscious Mexican girls. "I've heard it's pretty wild. Men have got themselves killed there."

"Quite a few, Major." Drury shut his eyes to what awaited him in Tucson. "Quite a few. Some bad, some good. A bullet doesn't know the difference. Nor a hang-rope."

Behind the ambulance, Sergeant O'Trist muttered hushedly to Linley, "Missy, what d'you think of him?"

"What do you expect me to say, Sarge? He's my cousin."

"Uh, yeah." He held his hands rigidly to his sides: lonely old soldier in love with a girl young enough to be his daughter. "Everything he does is right. Right as rain. Saved my life. Killed an Apache hand-to-hand. An' all the rest what he's done. Sure."

"What more can you ask, then?" she questioned. "What's bothering you, Sarge?"

"Missy, I can't get over the feeling he's a wrong-un!"

"You're just prejudiced." She didn't realize that the sergeant was in love with her, that he was jealously protective. All her life she had been accustomed to the friendship of soldiers—veteran noncoms, usually, who appointed themselves as her guardians. She had led a

70

sheltered life surrounded by men whose morals, where she was concerned, were sterner than the strictures of a pack of maiden aunts.

"He don't ring right to me, Missy. There's something bogus about him."

"He's my cousin," she reiterated.

"That don't make him no angel," O'Trist said doggedly. "Where's he been all these years? What's he been doin'? He knows Apaches—knows 'em too well for a white man!" He scanned her face shrewdly. "I fancy you've got the same feeling about him as I've got. Am I right?"

"No, no, Sarge!"

"Yeah." He nodded. "You've got it, only you won't say so! The major thinks Mr. Ken's a pure gift from heaven. We don't! Maybe he's a curse from hell, to lead us astray! Let's you an' me keep our eye on him!"

"Sergeant!" came the major's call.

O'Trist ducked around the ambulance. "Here, sir."

"Prepare to move out. We'll retrace east out of these mountains and head north for Tucson. Mr. Royal will guide us."

"Mr.—?"

"My nephew."

O'Trist whooshed a breath. "Pardon, sir, are we sure he'll keep us on the right route?"

"Mr. Royal knows what he is doing," said the major. "We will follow his guidance, every step, and pay close heed to his advice at all times. Is that clear, Sergeant?"

"Yes, sir."

"In case you're unhappy with that arrangement, I'm sure Corporal Lagerfeld can take over your duties. Do you wish to be relieved?"

"No, sir."

"Very well."

Sometimes, during the spells of bleak despondency that visit all solitary men, Jim Drury told himself that people, by and large, were unsatisfactory creatures. And worldly success, wealth, was an empty prize not worth the striving.

It didn't, of course, lighten the heavy mood. He then would make the effort to recall, sardonically, sweetly sad old songs heard in childhood. To poke fun at them. To twist their tenderest passages into hilarious ribaldry. But too often they got under his skin, damn them, and drove him to drinking. His drinking bouts were fantastic while they lasted. He had always taken everything to extremes, headlong and reckless of his own fate, yet curiously careful of the welfare of other people, those unsatisfactory creatures.

The first night after leaving the pass he came upon Linley seated on the tongue of the baggage wagon. The forty-odd soldiers were camped in Palo Alto at the end of a march of barely twenty miles for the day. The settlement was deserted, like others, everybody fleeing north from the Apache marauders.

She was picking inexpertly at the strings of a half-size guitar. Discovering him watching her, she said, "The lieutenant who gave me this vowed I was musical. How wrong he was! I can't play it to save my soul. Can you?"

"A little. Very little." A Mexican cow hand had once taught him a few basic chords. He took the guitar from her and ran a fingernail across the strings. "That lieutenant should have showed you how to tune it."

She smiled. "He couldn't play it, either. He brought it back from leave as a present for me."

The smile lighting her face transfigured it. Drury was standing above her tuning the guitar, and she tilted her head back to look up at him. Awareness then struck him, like a silent explosion, that she was intensely female, provocative. Suddenly the warm nearness of her presence was a torment. He was sure that she knew of it, which meant she knew her way among men. She was not the chilly young lady, prematurely old-maidish, that she appeared. Definitely not, this bright-eyed beauty whose every breath swelled the shape of womanly breasts beneath her blouse.

Was she, he wondered, purposely challenging him? Leading him on into some kind of booby trap? Two could play that game.

Experimentally, he strummed a sonorous chord. It sounded about right. He didn't hold any high opinion of his singing voice as a mating influence, so he murmured in a lilt the words of an old song, while brushing the strings in accompaniment. The song, nostalgic and anguished, was one of those that he had cynically paraphrased, parodied into bawdy doggerel. He did not parody it now, but husked the words straight, looking down at the girl seated on the tongue of the baggage wagon, hugging her knees and gazing up at him.

> *Soft in my heart*
> *You rest, beloved.*
> *Sunlight breaks the shade,*
> *Gilds the dark grass—*
> *Then once more I see you,*
> *See your smile.*
> *And I live on with you*
> *Soft in my heart.*

He stopped, remembering no more than that much of

it, touched in spite of himself by its sincere sentiment. For a moment he thought he had overplayed, made a fool of himself. Women were actually less sentimental then men, on the whole. They were the realists, discarding yesterday, seeking tomorrow.

The girl sat very still. Her eyes, looking up into his, were wide and deep as if astonished. A pulse beat visibly just forward of her left ear. Her lips were slightly parted and full, red. Her breasts rose stronger.

"That was beautiful!" She said it slowly, almost shyly. "Sadly beautiful. A love song to one who's gone. No, don't play anymore. Not after that." She came to her feet.

He thought she was blushing but he couldn't be sure. Starlight, from a billion stars in the blue-black sky, bleached colors to pearl-gray hues. The moon had not yet risen. Certainly the glow in her eyes couldn't be mistaken. He dropped the guitar and drew her to him.

She came swiftly and readily into his arms, passionate and unafraid of her emotions. He kissed her hard, his searching hands strongly fondling her. Something had triggered it, the equivalent of a bomb going off. She pressed herself to him, gasping, unashamedly encouraging his hands to explore her firm young body.

Then the harried, guilt-stricken whisper: "Darling, we mustn't! We're cousins!"

He murmured something smotheredly, face buried in her wealth of hair.

"Ken! We're first cousins! It—it would be like incest! Almost like brother and sister!"

He released her with wrenching regret. Desperately, he verged on telling her that he was no kin of hers whatever.

A cold thought intruded. Could that be her purpose? Lure him into confessing that he was an impostor? She had been suspicious of him, as had Sergeant O'Trist, from the start. They could have put their heads together and figured out this way of exposing him, playing upon his urgent virility. In which case, Linley had been merely acting a part.

"Thanks for your company, cousin," he said politely to her. "Don't forget your guitar."

She fled to the ambulance.

Returning from posting out relief pickets at midnight, the tireless Sergeant O'Trist stopped beside Drury, lying awake in a borrowed blanket. "It's quiet," he remarked for an opener, and Drury let a grunt serve as reply.

There was no denying the quietness. The adobe shacks of the abandoned village stood ghostly in the moonlight. Not even a mongrel dog was left to bark at the soldiers, whose snoring made the only sound. The restriction on smoking had been lifted; the sergeant fired up a short clay pipe, cupping the match closely in his palms although there was no wind. "Smoke?"

"Think I will." Drury stuffed and lit the small briar that he had salvaged from Kenneth Claude Royal's belongings. He reclined on one elbow, smoking, waiting for the sergeant to unburden himself of what preyed on his mind. "Why don't you sit down? Tough march tomorrow."

O'Trist did so. Presently, he asked, "Reckon you'll get us to Tucson?"

"I'm sure trying to."

"Yeah. You're doing a right good job, so far. I got no complaints on that score."

"Then what's your gripe?"

The directness of Drury's question threw the sergeant a bit off-balance. He tamped his clay pipe, emptied ashes, puffed, giving himself time for words that didn't come easily.

"Putting it plain—plain as you ask me—there's too much mystery about you. Too much that ain't explained!"

"Like what?"

"A federal lawman slogging through this country— why? You know Apaches. Christ, do you know 'em! How? There we was, blinding off into the blue and you showed up! Where from?"

"It was a coincidence," Drury said. "A happenstance. Troops are scattered. I was helping Lagerfeld's bunch and we happened on your outfit. That's all."

Unsatisfied, the sergeant grimaced. "It don't answer the questions. Maybe you're the major's nephew, I dunno. He says so."

"Do you doubt his word?"

"No. I just doubt he knows much more about you than I know, which ain't much. You got a trick of turning off questions about yourself. Another thing—"

"What?"

"Keep your hands off Missy. Miss Linley. The major's daughter. Leave her be."

Drury's eyes glinted. "Don't threaten me!"

"That's a threat, all right." Sergeant O'Trist knocked out his pipe. He got to his feet. "I'll kill you," he said, and paced off.

CHAPTER NINE

Heading his platoon the following day, the sergeant unslung his rifle startledly at sight of a bloodily disfigured face that poked up from behind a clump of dusty huisache. "Apache!"

"A squaw," Drury said. "Call a halt." He strode forward while the sergeant, rifle ready, grudgingly ordered the halt.

Major Royal climbed down from the ambulance, Linley helping him. "What is it?"

"An Apache squaw, sir," answered O'Trist. "So *he* says. They all look the same to me."

"Take his word for it, Sergeant."

"It might be a trick, sir. An ambush."

"He'd know if it was."

Corporal Lagerfeld spoke up. "He sure would, sir!"

The sergeant scowled. He sought to meet Linley's eyes, to exchange a meaningful glance of joint distrust. But her eyes were on Drury, watching him at the clump of huisache, watching him extend his hand ever so gently to the crouching, frightened squaw. The sergeant sighed heavily. They had all fallen under the spell of that mystery-shrouded man. Even Linley, at last.

The Apache squaw was young. Possibly she had been pretty before her lord and master slashed off her nose and left her to perish in the blazing heat—punishment for serious dereliction in domestic affairs, usually adultery. She was understandably bitter about it.

She hissed volubly to Drury of her grievance, finding that he could speak Apache. As to the cause of the horrible penalty, she was reticent, but he gained the impression that she was ripping mad at her lover for letting it happen to her. Never more would she be pretty and desirable. She hated her lover, her husband, her tribe.

"I'll take care of her, poor thing," Linley offered.

"Wait a minute," Drury said.

"She's suffering, can't you see?"

"You bet I see it!"

"Then—"

"She's in the mood now to give us information. Later on she won't be. We've got ourselves to think of!" He put rapid queries to the miserable young squaw. The semidisciplined green soldiers, breaking ranks without permission, gathered around to listen to the jabber, unintelligible to them.

The squaw's ready replies set Drury aback, making him realize the extent and unique force of the Apache uprising. He looked at Major Royal.

"She says a relief column is coming from Fort Thomas. Horse soldiers. An army. Would that be possible?"

"It's possible," the major granted. "Our recent trouble with Mexico—we've strengthened a garrison or two —Fort Thomas? That would be Colonel Broussard. Correction—Brevet-Brigadier General Broussard." A tinge of wry humor edged the major's voice. "He was breveted last year."

"There wasn't any war last year."

"He won his brevet in Washington. Before the shake-up."

Brevet rank, as far as Drury knew, was honorary rank, somewhat empty, conferred without a corresponding increase of pay. He said, "The Apaches are all gathering to bust up his army, this woman says."

"She must be crazy—or they are! A pack of skinny savages break an American army? Ridiculous!"

Drury thought of the skinny desert-tribesmen, knowing their tremendous endurance and lightning speed, their unpredictable flashes of berserk recklessness: an example being the charging warrior on the bank of the pass, mouthing his death song. He spoke once more to the squaw. She, covering her mutilated face with both hands against the morbid curiosity of the soldiers, replied in muffled monosyllables, already beginning to regret divulging so much to the white man.

"They're going to try, Major," he said. "It's the only reason why the Apaches around us sloped off as they did. To join the rest, the main bunch. Someone's in top command of 'em all."

"Who would that be?"

"She can't tell me. Or she won't. And I can't guess."

"The Drury renegade, perhaps?"

Again the cold mice-feet running up and down his spine. The tingling scalp. The stab of remembrance that he was a fraud, a much-wanted-man, impersonating a man who was dead. "Whoever it is, he's sending out the orders. First smash the cavalry. Then wipe out the pockets of foot soldiers. After that, the ranchers and settlers. The towns. Loot and burn them. Drive the white captives like animals down to the Apache *rancherias* in Mexico—where they won't be the first to taste slavery in its worst form!"

"My dear Ken, you draw a hideous picture!" protested the major. "It seems strange, coming from you!"

"This is a strange year. The Apaches have been preparing for it, in Mexico as well as the Arizona Territory. Folks living along the border have felt it coming."

"But in Washington—"

"Washington's a long way off. It takes them forever to vote an appropriation. Pork-barrel politicians block any measure that doesn't promise them a pay-off. What do they care? Their scalps are safe!"

"I'll try to make her comfortable in the baggage wagon," Linley said, drawing the squaw to her feet.

"Which means," Drury commented, "we'll have fleas in our blankets!"

Her look was scorching. "Must you say that?"

"It's the truth. She's a *rancheria* Apache. Their Mexican *rancherias* are stick-and-mud hovels in the brush. Hidden. They're fuller of fleas than a tramp dog."

"I'll take the chance!"

"Oh, bully for you, honey! But how about us?"

They were all scratching themselves next day on the northward march when the sergeant hailed to Drury, "What's wrong? Hostiles?" He was haunted by misgivings about this march, this route through trackless desert-country, guided by a man he personally disliked and distrusted.

It wasn't a march, by Army standards. The infantrymen shambled out of step on blistered feet. A glumly weary mob, short of water, food, ammunition. Come a surprise attack, an ambush, only God knew the outcome. Men could push themselves, or be pushed, only so far. There was a limit where life no longer mattered much. The sergeant knew that, he had soldiered under Sherman in Georgia.

His feelings about Drury were contrarily ambivalent. On the one hand, Drury had saved his life. He had to be thankful. On the other hand, the sergeant couldn't rid himself of his instinctive sense of distrust. The fact, too, that Linley was drawn to the tall man, regardless of how unwillingly, weighted O'Trist's dislike.

He hailed again, inserting a parade-ground bark to his voice, "What's wrong?"

Drury was returning from scouting forward and all around. He raised his right hand reassuringly, unwittingly, to the sergeant—an Indian gesture that the sergeant noted—and paced on to the ambulance. Major Royal, seated beside the driver, raised a haggard and unshaven face to him.

"Yes, Ken? Trouble?"

"No. Rather the reverse." Drury glimpsed Linley's face peering from between the split canvas curtains of the ambulance. He raised his battered hat to her. "Major, a squad of cavalry is coming up on us. A small squad, eight or ten riders. Behind us, from the southeast."

"Good Lord!" The major stared. "They must be lost!" He raised his voice. "Sergeant! Halt!"

"I don't think they're lost," Drury said. "They ride too well in formation. I think they've got a message for you and they're hurrying to deliver it."

"What message could they have? We're here in the middle of nowhere!"

"We'll soon know. Here they come."

It was a corporal's squad, led by an aging captain whose face seemed permanently sunk into lines of disillusionment, probably aggravated by dyspepsia. The mounted troopers, dust-laden and plainly tired, brisked up at the sight of Linley, but their officer paid her only a juiceless glance.

81

Dismounting stiffly, he exchanged salutes and introductions with Major Royal. He was Captain Gaylord, Third Cavalry, attached to General Broussard's relief column. He pronounced the title of general with dour distinctness, as if in ironic deference to the bearer of it, omitting the depreciative prefix of Brevet-Brigadier.

Major Royal understood the intonation as well as the captain's resigned discontent. These days, the Civil War belonging safely to the past, the Army was an unpopular orphan, penny-pinched, a skeleton force. Onetime commanders of proud regiments were now serving on as junior officers. They didn't mind that too greatly, so many of them being in the same boat. What griped them was that promotion could sometimes be won through political influence, family position, by knowing and being known by the right people.

"How did you know where to find us?" the major asked.

Captain Gaylord replied that an Apache, captured in a skirmish, had revealed the information. "General Broussard then detailed me to find you. You are to proceed with all possible speed to join the relief column."

"Mr. Gaylord, these men are not in any condition to make a forced march! We're trying to reach Tucson."

The captain appeared to manage his face carefully as if its dry skin might split if he changed expression. "It is an order, sir. General Broussard is senior officer in command of emergency operations at present."

"But my daughter is with me!" protested the major. "She must have an escort to Tucson!"

"General Broussard," the captain droned, "made no possible exceptions to his order. The order is explicit. It requires you to report to him with all men at your disposal, conditions regardless—the general's own words, not mine."

"On pain of court martial, I suppose?"

"That was implied." For an instant the frozen face showed a tinge of human concern. "If I may offer my opinion, your daughter will be far safer with the relief column than if you persist in trying to take her to Tucson. I'm afraid you'd never make it."

"Why?"

"According to the Apache we took prisoner, the devils have poisoned the wells and waterholes."

"My God! And our water's nearly gone!"

"Bands of hostiles are raiding the outskirts of Tucson itself, we're told. The town's in a state of siege, with the Camp Lowell garrison badly undermanned. The Apaches are everywhere."

Drury put a question, one that had nagged at him since he first sighted the cavalry squad. "Didn't you run into any trouble, getting here to us? Apache trouble, I mean."

Captain Gaylord spared him a fleeting glance. Then, on second look, a trace of curiosity kindled in his eyes. "None. We knew, though, that some of them were trailing us, watching us. They didn't attack."

"That's odd."

"Yes, it is. Not a shot. Who're you? Haven't I met you before? You look strangely familiar. And yet—"

"My nephew," the major broke in. "Kenneth Claude Royal, U.S. Deputy marshal. Mr. Gaylord, I see no option but to obey General Broussard's order. If you'll lead us to the relief column—"

"That's what I'm here for, sir."

The footsore infantrymen groaned.

They shambled in silence under the blazing sun, dispirited, too fatigue-drugged to curse their bad luck. Men stumbled against each other, fell, reached down for dropped rifles and fell again. The mules drawing the ambulance and baggage wagon, overworked and underfed, sullenly kicked at anyone coming near them. At every halt they slipped out of the collars and tangled the harness. Halts had to be frequent, for rest and to let stragglers catch up. The cavalrymen constantly had to rein in their horses and wait.

"When I pulled the Tres Santos tour of duty," Major Royal told Drury, "I had a feeling it wouldn't be easy. A premonition. I laid my uneasiness to the fact that I'd been comfortably settled too long in a snug post. The Army shake-up, I told myself, was a good thing for old barracks-bugs like me. Get some of us out of our humdrum ruts. Knock the rust off us."

He laughed wryly. "If my premonition had let me know what I was really in for, I'd have resigned my commission! Oh, well, optimism—hope—is fortune's rigged lottery that cheats us all, eventually, death having the winning ticket. Don't you want to ride up here and rest your legs for a while?"

Drury, striding alongside the ambulance, shook his head. The infantrymen were walking as best they could, expecting no favors. "My legs are okay."

"So I've noticed. Long and strong, typical of our family. You've inherited the best traits, Ken."

Shifting away from that guilty subject, Drury asked, "What do you know about General Broussard? What kind of man if he? He seems, h'm, severe."

It took the major a long time to reply. Had the query come from a fellow officer, he would have snubbed it off. At last he said, letting down, "When I was a captain, company commander, Broussard served under me as a lieutenant. I reprimanded him once for incompetence, and another time for incipient insubordination. His attitude was extremely arrogant—due, no doubt, to his family ties. The Broussards were a power in Washington. Still are, though perhaps not as much now."

"You didn't hit it off with him."

"That's putting it mildly. It was the final year of the War, before he struck his transfer to cavalry and went on up by the Washington route—family power, money, politics. I wouldn't have recommended him for promotion to platoon leader!"

"And that's General Broussard, commander of emergency operations of war? God help us!"

"That," said the major correctingly, "is Colonel Broussard, Brevet-Brigadier General by the grace of corrupt influence! Our leader, to whom we're now inching our way. As you say, Ken—God help us!"

Why, Drury speculated, had the watchful Apaches allowed Captain Gaylord's squad to come through? He knew by instinct that the Apaches were still intently on watch, all around in the low hummocks and sand dunes. Was it actually possible that they were controlled and disciplined by a supreme mastermind?

Let the fish swim into the net. The paleface fish. The cavalry and the heap-walk soldiers. And the white woman. All in one grand coup. Draw the net tight, slaughter the soldiers, make sport with the woman—

"Are you cold, in this heat?" the major asked. "You shivered!"

"Somebody walked over my grave," Drury said. "Is it possible that Broussard knows you're the officer who's in charge of this outfit?"

"He may have guessed. He must have been briefed on what officers and troops are in this district."

"Scattered to hell now, though, a good many! Some dead. Tres Santos is gone."

"True. But we're still roughly in the district. Given a thorough briefing and a topographical map of the terrain, it's not hard to estimate the probable positions of displaced troops—that is, contingents of troops like this, not the stray individuals, you understand. Discipline holds an army together and with it you can calculate the actions—marches and countermarches—of any segment of it, anywhere."

Drury hid his eyes, absolutely dissenting. Holy Heaven, were these soldiers counted merely as numbers, nameless parts, cogs of a machine controlled by mindless rote and rule? These were men he had fought alongside, knowing them as individuals, knowing their names, nicknames: Jake, Scotty, Four Eyes, all the rest.

"Major, would Broussard still be nursing a grudge against you after these years? Would it account for his goddam order that you must report to him, 'conditions regardless'?"

"It is possible."

"Would he, for that grudge, risk his relief column? We're not in any shape to go into battle! What you've got here are worn-out men. And you're wounded. Would he?"

Again it took the major a long time to answer. He removed his hat and scrubbed his sweat-plastered hair. He glanced at the ambulance driver beside him, who watched sourly the fractious mules. He leaned down confidentially to Drury and lowered his voice.

"I'm not the only one, Ken. Broussard is in a position to pay off old scores. He collected many. Captain Gaylord is one, I suspect. It's the Army game, the way it's played nowadays. Top dog bites little dog!"

"He would—?"

"I'm afraid he would!"

CHAPTER TEN

General Broussard stepped out from his tent only after the infantry detachment shuffled to a halt in the encampment and he did it with an air of regal condescension. The tardiness of his greeting could be construed only as an intentional snub, for the outlying pickets surely had reported the slow advance of the oncoming detachment. He'd had plenty of time to extend the ordinary courtesies—a ready welcome, a wry joke or two, a drink.

He was very tall and thin. His uniform was immaculate, thanks to anxious orderlies. Boots glossy. Brass buttons shining. Spotless gloves tucked in belt. The narrowness of his face was accentuated by his cavalry-fashion mustache and tuft of beard, waxed to dagger points. The small beard, carefully cultivated and trimmed, lent his chin a thrusting quality.

Excessively verging on caricature, he presented the epitome of the indomitable cavalry commander. Consciously. But any man who was a real man could see through him, could puncture his facade and know he was a fake. Good commanding officers don't pull rank.

Broussard, pulling rank, acknowledged with a haughty nod Major Royal's correct salute. He didn't even raise a finger to his brow but surveyed contemptuously the infantrymen.

Dazed by exhaustion they leaned against one another. A scruffy, worn-out bunch. The resting cavalrymen of the encampment looked at them with heartfelt sympathy, knowing what they must have gone through. Some of them offered tobacco and hardtack. The worn-out infantrymen mumbled their thanks and sank to earth.

"That's a sorry lot of wobblers you've brought to me, Mr. Royal! More a liability than an asset!"

The major's haggard face flared red. "These are soldiers! They've fought and marched for days on short rations!"

"Excuses not accepted!" snapped Broussard. His eyes were pale blue, small. He gave force to them by staring frostily.

"I remind you that it was by your order that we marched to join your relief force," said the major.

"Relief force? Nonsense! I'm commanding an army and my purpose is to put down the Apaches—wherever and whenever I meet them!"

Broussard had never met face-to-face an Apache warrior, Drury guessed. Surrounded by hundreds of cavalry troopers, an army, Broussard believed himself a conquering Napoleon. He actually and obviously believed it.

"The scrawny curs will get a lesson they'll never forget, when I hunt them down!" he vowed, implying contempt for the major's detachment for taking a mauling from scrawny curs. "You don't seem to have made much of a showing against them, Mr. Royal, judging from your condition!"

The major's forebodings, Drury reflected, were being fully realized. Worse—far worse than venting spleen upon a fellow officer who had once been his superior— was Broussard's inexperience coupled with overblown confidence. He exposed his ignorance by his sweeping scorn of Apaches as scrawny curs. They were scrawny, all chest and skinny limbs, but Indian-fighters never underestimated them.

By mischance and behind-scene influence, the Army

shake-up had placed an ego-inflated man in command of this column. An incompetent blowhard whose word was law.

Evidently conscious of Drury's silent criticism, Broussard pinned an antagonistic stare on him. "Who's this man?"

Major Royal, white-lipped with controlled wrath, replied, "Mr. Kenneth C. Royal, a U.S. deputy marshal. My nephew. An expert guide and scout. I recommend him as your—"

Broussard cut him off. "I've got a scout. The best. You can offer me nothing I need!"

"Your discourtesty, sir, insults me and my men! At the proper time I shall request a court of inquiry!"

"Indeed! And I shall then charge you with incompetence and incipient insubordination! Your attitude, Mr. Royal, challenges my authority! Grounds for a court martial!"

"My record is clear, Mr. Broussard. My conduct—"

"General Broussard, Mr. Royal! Stand corrected! I'm General Broussard, commandant!" The haughty pulling of rank shamed the title.

"Colonel Broussard, Brevet-Brigadier," returned the major with cutting distinctness, "I do not need reminding of your superior rank. I remember you as a lieutenant in those past days when comradely courtesy prevailed."

"Is that an apology?"

"No, General, it is an explanation."

The friction between the two officers was electric and made them utterly irreconcilable. They detested each other.

The Apache woman peeped out timidly from the baggage wagon. Her mutilated face, bandaged by Lin-ey, was a grotesque mask, stringy hair hanging over it—the woman had made a pitifully feminine attempt to hide her noseless condition.

Catching sight of her, Broussard demanded, "What the devil is that creature?"

"A squaw we picked up," the major answered. "Hurt by her own people. She gave us information."

"Get rid of her!"

"But she's—"

"At once! We're not giving aid and comfort to Apaches! No accommodation for prisoners! Run her off!"

"General Broussard," said Drury with forced civility, "it is my understanding that you have a prisoner, an Apache warrior, captured in a skirmish."

"He's dead. I had him shot."

"Too bad. He might have let spill some more information. I can speak Apache."

Broussard flapped a hand dismissingly. "Not needed. I don't wish to hear what any savage has to say. Mr. Royal—" he made the same dismissing gesture to the major—"Captain Gaylord will show you where to camp your men." The gesture was in itself a deliberate insult. "We move out at daybreak."

Containing his anger, Major Royal said, "I bring to your attention the fact that my daughter is with me. I am much concerned with seeing her safely to Tucson."

Something like satisfaction entered the pale eyes. "The fact is unfortunate, but of your own doing, no concern of mine! By Army regulations, unenlisted persons rate as campfollowers. I can't spare an escort for your daughter, and I doubt if your men could march that distance."

"Nor can my men march tomorrow with this column! Their boots are in shreds! Their feet—"

"I'll give them permission to mount our spare

horses," Broussard said condescendingly. "We march at daybreak." Liking the phrase, he repeated it, adding embellishments. "We march on at daybreak to meet and crush the enemy!" Grand words, resoundingly delivered. He should have gone on the stage, Drury thought, where he could do no harm.

"Thank you, sir. Most generous of you." Major Royal barely succeeded in restraining his bitter irony. "However, *sir,* some of my men probably can't ride—else they wouldn't have joined the infantry."

"Let them learn! This is a cavalry column. The function of cavalry is to move fast and attack! I don't tolerate laggards and gold-brickers in my command!" Broussard twirled his waxed mustache-points, gazing loftily into the distance, no doubt seeing himself as the hero of Arizona, loaded with medals, promoted to full general by an applauding Congress. Commander-in-chief of the district. "We march at daybreak!"

"May I ask where?"

"I'll tell you when I see fit. Camp your men!"

After dark, Drury, restlessly sleepless, made his way toward the ambulance. All around, the big camp spread quiet, men slumbering, horses dozing in tether with saddles lying stacked within ready reach. Once in a while came a mutter from pickets boredly accosting one another on their rounds. In the moonlight Broussard's tent, his command post, was a ghostly cone, the guidon hanging unstirred in the windless night. The train of supply wagons was drawn in a ring, with ropes stretched between, forming a corral for the mule teams. No light showed, by strict order—a senseless order, for the ever-watching Apache spies certainly knew everything about the camp, its strength and arrangement, every detail of it.

Seated on the tongue of the ambulance, Major Royal raised a lighted cigar in greeting. "Sorry I can't offer you one. This is my last cigar. Been saving it for an emergency."

"I saw the glow of it. Noticed you were smoking pretty fast. Mind my company?"

"Glad. I've been trying to compose myself, settle my mind. Anger, according to Pythagoras, begins in folly and ends in repentance. Self-destructive. Sit down. I feel better already."

Drury sat. He stuffed his pipe and lighted it. " 'Beware of the fury of a patient man,' " he quoted.

"That was Dryden, wasn't it?"

"Damned if I remember. I read it somewhere, sometime. It stuck. One of those things."

"I know. Like my scraps of philosophy."

"Let's quit beating around the bush," Drury said. "What's on our minds is Broussard! A hollow man, nothing inside him but a froth of bile and bullhead arrogance! Do you have any idea where he figures to lead this so-called army of his?"

The major took time to tap ash from his cigar. "Your language is immoderate. I can't engage you in those terms. General Broussard is my superior, at present my commander."

"Forget it for a minute, will you? Between us? Nobody else is listening." Nobody except Linley inside the ambulance. Drury sensed that she was awake, listening to his voice, and suddenly a craving for her shook and choked him. He imagined her as she was, in a night gown, flimsy garment discarded willingly.

"All right, Ken." The major uttered a muted laugh. "All right! Thank God, I've got you to remind me I'm human, not a cog in a soulless machine! To answer your question—no, Broussard has not confided to me his plans. He never will, I imagine. Not until the last hour, anyway, or when campaign procedure requires him to call his officers together for final conference—and he might shut me out of that, I not being actually a member of his staff."

"Do we go blinding off to an unknown destination, then? Led by a puffed-up greenhorn who's ignorant of the country? Saints preserve us!"

"It isn't quite that bad, Ken." The major drew hard on his diminishing cigar and exhaled. "I had a talk with Captain Gaylord. A good man under his sour crust, Broussard's scout is out ahead with a small party of Indian friendlies—on pay, of course—scouting the route. Been out a couple of days, sending back reports. So we're not blinding off into the blue, you see."

"Where *are* we blinding off to?" Drury asked him. "Did the captain tell you?"

"Yes. Broussard intends to stroke at the heart of the enemy. Their headquarters, so to speak, where their ammunition and orders come from, according to his scout."

"What's the name of it?"

"Apache Rocks. It's a daring objective."

"Daring, hell!" Drury exclaimed. "It's suicidal! Apache Rocks, up the mountains from Cave Creek Canyon—I know that goddam hell-trap! It's also called the Chiricahua Stronghold. Way back, Spanish *conquistadores* got lost and slaughtered in it. And troops since then. The Chiricahua Stronghold can't be taken by this fumbling column, give you my word! Horses are useless there."

"Broussard's scout assures him it can be taken," said the major. "A strong attack, a cavalry charge—"

94

"Crap! In the Chiricahua Stronghold you can't charge. Too many rocks. His scout's a fool if he thinks otherwise. Who is he, do you know?"

"He's famous, Ken. Top scout. Broussard's lucky to have him. He's no other than Harl Soderman."

Drury bit down hard on the stem of his pipe. "Oh?"

The gods of chance, he reflected, had loaded the dice against him, from the hour he crossed back north over the border. He had known the risk. His friends, the Bloodstoner Apaches, had tried to dissuade him from leaving their valley. Although long Christianized, the Bloodstoners still retained that ancient gift of prescience, called animal instinct by Kenneth C. Royal, U.S. deputy marshal: a misty foreknowledge, a warning awareness of what lay waiting over the next ridge.

Logically, he reflected further, he shouldn't be too shocked by the news that Harl Soderman was Broussard's scout. After all, in the relatively sparse population of the Arizona Territory, the same men cropped up again and again in emergency. Soderman wouldn't be left out.

"Ken, do you know Soderman?"

"I met him once."

At that violent meeting two years ago at the ant hills, Drury had outlawed himself by shooting the famous scout in the neck. Two soldiers killed in the ensuing fracas between the military and the savages, Drury gunning on the savage's side. Renegade. A white man taking up for redmen.

"Really? You've actually met Soderman, that legendary figure?" the major asked, impressed.

Drury reverted to the language of his father." 'Deed, aye! I know him, and he knows me."

Soderman wouldn't have overlooked that bullet through his neck, wouldn't have forgotten the man who inflicted it. He knew Drury's true identity as a mustanger, prospector, trapper, a Southwestern tramp handy with guns. Not, decidedly not, as Kenneth C. Royal, U.S. law officer.

"I guess you'll enjoy renewing old acquaintance with Soderman," commented the major with a touch of envy.

"Oh, sure," Drury lied. "When is he expected to drop back and join the column?"

"I've no idea. It would have to be before we get to Apache Rocks, for him to give a final report to Broussard."

"Yeah. At least a day before."

That offered time to slip away and quit the column. Let the column go smash to smithereens in the Chiricahua Stronghold, under its vainglorious commander. He, Drury, could get back to Mexico, make his way regardless of Apache warparties, could outstalk and outshoot any in his way.

But the column contained Jake Lagerfeld and nigh on forty junipers who relied on Drury—Ken—as leader. It contained Linley, Major Royal, all the rest of them. Drury sighed heavily, staring into a dark and private pit of hopelessly insoluable problems.

CHAPTER ELEVEN

The column advanced in trim order, Broussard a strikingly gallant-looking figure at its head, campaign hat tilted to a swank slant, hands gloved, gold epaulets and double row of eighteen brass buttons gleaming. His mount, a handsome white horse which he rode with conscious pride and erectness, had been carefully schooled as a five-gaited saddler.

He must have bought that horse out of his own pocket, Drury surmised. A costly horse, worth a year's pay or more. Not the kind of bucking broomtail that came with Army remounts. It wouldn't throw an old lady. A gentleman horse, well mannered.

But white? A white horse, said Mexicans and others who knew horses, lacked stamina and fell prey to diseases too easily. Not only that, white horses were conspicuous, they showed up in the dark when a rider wished to be unseen. White horses were for show-offs.

Behind Broussard, at correct parade-ground distance, half a horse's length, rode Captain Gaylord and two other junior officers. Very junior: Broussard never unbent to consult with them. Captain Gaylord, ostensibly adjutant, knew practically nothing about his superior's plan of attack—if a plan existed, which Gaylord doubted.

And back of them rode the column of cavalry and mounted infantry, the supply train of wagons trundling in the rear with the essential supplies and ammunition. The small force of mounted infantry rode clumsily, all worn-out, most of them townies or farm boys, unfamiliar with saddles and stirrups.

The column possessed no artillery whatever, not one mortar piece with which to lob explosive shells at the Indians, who had a healthy fear of them. Cavalry formed the backbone and body of this army.

General Broussard, undefeatable military genius would, by God, show the recalcitrant Apaches the devastating power of his cavalry. Smash them. Make the scurvy curs toe the line, humbly and quick-sharp. Other Army commanders had gone too easy on them in the past, been weakly tolerant. General Broussard would make no such mistake. Ever.

He turned stiffly in his saddle. "Mr. Gaylord!" He had adopted a parade-ground trick used by drill sergeants, of pulling the chin in tight, making the voice deeper and more chestily resonant.

"Yes, sir?"

"We should soon be reaching our objective."

Privately disagreeing, Captain Gaylord said nothing. By then the column had begun winding up into the mountains. Higher mountains loomed farther on, craggy and forbidding. The Apaches surely wouldn't make their stand down here, when that jumble of high peaks invited them. They had the lungs to breathe easily the thin air of high altitudes, a terrific advantage.

"Our objective," Broussard throated, chin pressing chest, "is Apache Rocks. Scout Soderman's messages to me are optimistic. We can sweep the enemy into a hole —with their leaders, chiefs and medicine men! Apache Rocks is their headquarters, which we will wipe out! Mr. Gaylord, pass my order back to the officers and men."

"Your order, sir?"

"They are to kill all Apache warriors, wherever found. We will burn their villages and destroy their ponies. We will take no prisoners!"

"Their women and children?"

Broussard dug his chin deeper. "Any of them found bearing weapons—so much as a knife—is to be shot!"

Gaylord took a breath. "I beg leave to call to your attention that in the articles of civilized warfare—"

"We're not dealing with a civilized enemy! You have my order! Deliver it to my command!"

"Yes, sir." Gaylord saluted and wheeled his horse.

When the order trickled back to the awkwardly riding infantry bunch, Drury exclaimed, "He's a goddam fool!"

Sergeant O'Trist heard him, as they all did. Corporal Lagerfeld nodded, open to take Drury's judgment on practically any matter. O'Trist, riding at the tailgate of the ambulance, in undertoned conversation with Linley, said loudly, "Mr. Civilian, you don't rate calling an officer that!"

He shook off Linley's restraining hand and reined his horse around. His big face flared, it bore the scars of countless brawls. "You don't rate a cussed thing in this man's army 'cept a bust in the jaw!"

"Want to try it?" Drury inquired.

"Ever since I first laid eyes on you, yeah!"

"I'll be ready for you when we make camp tonight. That be okay?"

"It's okay."

He wasn't ready that night. Chewing hardtack washed down with tepid water—no fires allowed—with Lagerfeld and some other sore-backsides, Drury did what he could to enliven low spirits with the telling of bawdy Indian jokes. Lagerfeld tried too late to warn him. A massive arm encircled Drury's neck, yanking him backward. A fist hooked him in the jaw.

"How'll that do for a start?" growled O'Trist, bringing his knee up for a spine-crippler.

"Dirty fighting!" Lagerfeld hissed. "Dirty Irish trick!"

His reflexes instantly triggered, Drury reached upward and rearward over his shoulders and got a lockhold on the sergeant's head. He had wrestled with Indian bucks for bets, deadly duels that knew no rules. Hunching his back, he heaved.

O'Trist sailed a somersault, legs waggling high in the air, but the reaction of a seasoned brawler enabled him to land rolling. Steadying to his hands and knees, he whooshed a breath in grudging tribute. The strength of tall, lean Royal surprised him. He knew very well that Royal could have broken O'Trist's neck by keeping hold of O'Trist's head in the toss.

The act of mercy increased the animosity that O'Trist had been building up against the man. O'Trist would not give Royal another such opportunity. He rose upright, balling his fists for battle. His good, big Irish fists, ever reliable. Sledgehammers. Be damned to wrassling, this bloody guy was too smart at it.

Deceptively indolent and casual, he set his stance before proceeding to mayhem. He hummed a bit of a boisterous County Galway song: *Up came McGinty, wid a coffin in each hand*—And abruptly he rushed, left arm and fist fully extended, the right bent ready to undercut. Fine style, approved by professional bareknucklers.

At the last fraction of an instant Drury ducked aside and hit O'Trist a scraping blow on the ear. Whirling around, O'Trist made for him again.

Lagerfeld's watching men crowed quietly. They expected Ken to leave his marks on the sergeant.

At the ambulance, Linley whispered to the major, "Put a stop to it! He'll kill him!"

"Who'll kill who?" her father asked. "Hush! I'm not supposed to see this."

Drury side-stepped and struck, aiming for the nose, to bring blinding tears to the eyes, but this time O'Trist saw it coming and he caught the punch on his forehead, purposely. It was like fisting a stone wall. The shock of it numbed Drury's hand.

He couldn't afford to repeat that error. Fast footwork saved him from an uppercut that missed his cheek by a hair. O'Trist's ferocious grin followed him. The sergeant was more than an ordinary brawling slugger, more crafty, although he did seem to depend largely on his terrific right swing. Maybe the left arm was muscle-bound. Drury footed to O'Trist's left side.

In a flash, the left arm retracted and shot forward like the oiled piston of a steam engine. It knocked Drury sprawled on his back in the dirt. Dazed, his head ringing, a lump swelling between his eyes, he scrambled up.

Lagerfeld and his men sighed, seeing him stumble. The corporal called out to O'Trist, stalking in for the kill, "Give him a chance, you dirty Irisher!"

O'Trist looked at him. "Jew man, be careful what you call me!" Hands on his hips, he asked Drury, "Had enough?"

"Nowhere near!"

"Okay, let's get at it! Quiet, you guys—we don't want no officers spoiling this, hear?"

"Dad, stop it!" Linley urged. "He's tired out, underfed, hurt!"

"You mean Ken?"

"Of course I mean Ken! Sarge is a bull. He'll kill him!"

"Ken isn't finished yet," said the major. "Want to bet? Give you two-to-five he ends on his feet."

Drury avoided O'Trist's rush, but a wide-arm swinger knocked him down again. He needed time to clear his head, to get himself coordinated, and O'Trist, knowing it, wouldn't allow him that respite. He saw O'Trist standing over him, a foot upraised to enforce the humiliation of stomping his face.

Black rage boiled up in him. It dissipated his cloudiness. He grabbed hold of the upraised foot and, rolling over, forced O'Trist to earth. Springing up, he booted O'Trist, while grating savagely, "Get up, you Goddam tater-gnawing skitter!" In that moment he was a barbarian and he looked it.

O'Trist bounded to his feet. "Skitter?" It had been a long time since he heard that word, a peculiarly offensive insult, to the Irish learned by Drury from his father. "Skitter, is it? I'll show you!"

"Come on!"

"Bloody Ulster prod!"

"Stinking papist!"

They closed in, slugging. Drury concentrated on O'Trist's middle and kept crowding, giving that piledriver left no room to uncork another long shocker. The sergeant, not at his best at in-fighting, and vulnerable to the punishing jabs, lost his wind and tried to break clear for a breather. Drury refused him the chance, keeping after him, thudding at his middle.

Gasping, O'Trist changed tactics and sought to grapple, to grasp hold of Drury and butt him in the face. Drury caught his outspread arms, wrenched them crosswise, and threw him with the assist of a knee in his stomach.

He stared down at O'Trist. Weariness then almost sank him. It was all he could do to brace his shaking legs. The hurts to his hands and battered body throbbed.

102

"I'm finished," he said to O'Trist. "Don't get up. I'd have to use my boots on you. It's something I don't like."

"I think that's about enough," Major Royal called from the ambulance. "Some of you men tend to the sergeant. Ken—"

"Yes, sir."

"Step over here. Peel off that shirt, what's left of it. Let's have a look at you—Lord! You're a mass of cuts and bruises, man. Linley—warm water. Liniment. Court plaster—"

"I'll take care of him," Linley said quietly.

"And a stiff drink. In the medical kit there's—"

"I said I'll take care of him."

"Eh? Oh, yes. Well, if you need help—"

"I don't. Come inside the ambulance, Ken."

CHAPTER TWELVE

At midnight, General Broussard unexpectedly issued an order calling for all officers to meet with him immediately. The officers scrambled out of bedrolls, affixed dress and hurried to obey the summons. They all knew, down to the second lieutenants, that Broussard's actual rank was colonel, that his higher rank of brevet brigadier was more-or-less honorary, given to him by virtue of political strings. Nevertheless, Broussard commanded this army and he was a hardnosed martinet. He wore the stars on his shoulders, enforcing upon everyone his supreme authority.

Against his own ruling, Broussard had a hurricane lamp burning brightly in front of his tent, in the middle of the camp.

"Gentlemen—"

His half-querying tone of voice made a sarcastic slur of the term, particularly aimed at those of the assembled officers who came from less than a prominent background, the few who somehow had managed by merit to win their commissions. He was infatuated with the outworn European model of an elite officer class. His own surname he pronounced elegantly as *Broussair*, which would have surprised his grandfather who had started the family fortune with a pushcart.

"Gentlemen, I am reliably informed that the enemy shows no signs of making active preparations for defense. They may know of our advance but they're not yet aware of our intention. They evidently feel secure—thanks to their experience with previous Army commanders who moved too cautiously and slowly against them, no doubt! *My* intention is to strike fast and catch them napping! We march to attack at dawn!"

Standing rearward of the grouped officers, out of the lantern light, Drury listened incredulously. Catch the Apaches napping? This blundering army that couldn't move without raising rumbles of sound and clouds of dust? Impossible.

"My plan is simple," Broussard continued. "Two hours' march will bring us to a place called Point of Rocks. Wagons can't proceed farther than that, due to the terrain. So our supply train halts there, with the sick and wounded, in our rear."

"Guarded?" inquired Captain Gaylord.

"By Major Royal and his contingent, in the unlikely event of an attack on it. You hear me, Mr. Royal?"

"I hear you, sir," replied the major.

"Very well! At Point of Rocks, two routes fork open for cavalry. Battalions A and B will take the upper route, under my personal command. All other units available will take the lower route, under Captain Gaylord. Any comments?"

"Sir," said Captain Gaylord civilly, "it means splitting the cavalry into two separate columns, probably without means of communication with each other. It is a risky maneuver."

"Soldiers in battle must take risks!" Broussard snapped, bristling at the invited criticism.

"Yes, sir. The column under my command will not be very strong. The terrain is unknown to me, except from hearsay. Perhaps Major Royal's nephew will consent to act as my guide."

"Humph! Any other comments, gentlemen?"

Major Royal spoke up. "I must agree with Captain Gaylord's misgivings. My nephew informs me that the terrain is unsuited to cavalry attack."

"Indeed!" Broussard's hatchet face flared. "Is your civilian nephew a military expert? Does he question my competence?"

"Not at all, sir. But he knows this country. He describes Apache Rocks as being virtually impossible for cavalry to penetrate, against an Apache defending force. It's called the Chiricahua Stronghold. Horses are useless there."

"He's a liar! My information is quite different, from a far better qualified source. Soderman, where are you? Step this way, please!"

Into the light of the hurricane lamp moved a man whose fringed buckskins contrasted with the blue uniforms. He had a long, thick body, the torso of a tall man, but his grotesquely short legs failed to bring him up to average height. Most men of his ill-proportioned build would have appeared ludicrous. He overcame the handicap by exerting a force of personality that made itself immediately felt. He had bulging brows, a broad nose, narrow lips. His heavy eyelids drooped, cowling the eyes to enigmatic slits. Respectful attention rippled through the assembly of officers.

"Soderman returned from scouting only a short while ago," Broussard announced, "which is why I called this meeting. He has given me his report. He will tell you the facts now, the true facts regarding—"

"Just a minute, Gen'l," Soderman stopped him, and it was a measure of his personality that Broussard bore the interruption with only a slight frown. "I heard the talk here," the scout said. "Who's the man claiming he knows the Chiricahua Stronghold?"

Before anyone spoke, he raised an arm and pointed straight at Jim Drury. "That him?"

Drury stood back in dark shadow, his presence unknown to any of the officers. He had thought to slip off

106

unobserved before the meeting ended. But Soderman, cat-eyed scout, had spotted him, was now pacing toward him, unceremoniously pushing a path through officers in his way.

He hoped the darkness, and the lumps he had garnered from Sergeant O'Trist's fists, would make him hard to recognize. After all, Soderman had only seen him once, and that was two years past, in the heat and scramble of the shooting fight at the ant hills.

Soderman confronted him. He reeked of antagonism, although his face was expressionless. Instead of raising his head to look up into Drury's face, he bent his body backward. "If you've been round this country so much, how's it we never met?" he queried.

Drury relaxed, grateful to O'Trist's pummeling knuckles. Major Royal, limping forward, said, "You met once, Ken told me. He's Ken Royal, my nephew."

Soderman looked around at the major. To do so he twisted his monstrous torso at the waist. It then became apparent that he had a permanently locked neck, making his head immovable. The action lent him an air of stilted dignity that was oddly impressive. He made an asset even of that handicap—a crippling injury which Drury guessed had been caused by his bullet.

"I never met any Ken Royal, far's I recall," Soderman said to the major. He twisted back swiftly. The point of a ten-inch blade prodded Drury's middle. The heavy-lidded eyes flashed open, wide and staring, colorless like oysters. "But I've sure met Drury once before! Renegade Drury! Don't move—I'll knife you up to your breastbone!"

The officers stood dumbfounded. Major Royal, choking with wrath, burst out, "You're insane! Ken's a federal marshal! Put your damned knife away!"

Soderman gaped his mouth in silent laughter. "Federal marshal! Him? That's rich! Federal marshals have been on the lookout for him a long time. So's the Army. And the Rangers—I heard they caught him and he got away."

"Rubbish! Ken has identification papers, credentials, everything. I examined them myself. That's when I discovered he was my nephew, Kenneth Claude Royal."

"You can bet he killed your nephew for 'em, then, because I know who he is! It was him shot me in the neck. Him and some Mexican Apaches jumped an Army escort I was guiding."

Broussard came stalking over from the hurricane lamp. His small eyes glittered. "What the devil is this? Soderman, did I hear you say this man is actually Renegade Drury?"

"The White Apache himself, Gen'l!"

"You're sure? Or is this a matter of personal enmity?"

"Plenty of personal enmity—plenty! But I'm dead sure." The knife in Soderman's grip pressed harder, pricking Drury through cloth and into flesh. "We've caught a big prize right here in your camp. Syping on you for the Apaches. Skulking in the dark, listening to your campaign plans. That ain't all."

"I—" Drury began.

"Silence!" Broussard thundered at him. The officers were regarding him gravely, stonily. All but Major Royal, who shook his head in angry distress for him. And Captain Gaylord whose severe face expressed doubt. "Go on, Soderman," said Broussard.

Soderman shrugged. "You can easy figure it y'self, Gen'l. He aimed to save his redskin friends from a licking. Or try. Anybody can see you're too much for 'em. So he spread lies about how the Chiricahua Stronghold couldn't be took by cavalry, no use trying. Guess he

108

hoped maybe to rattle you, make you change your plans. Hah! He don't know *you*, Gen'l!"

"He certainly doesn't!" Broussard agreed, tugging fiercely at his dagger-like cavalry mustache. "Mr. Gaylord! I order that man chained to a wagon, guarded every minute! No food or water!"

"Sir!" shouted Major Royal. "I protest such excessive punishment. It is unwarranted! I protest most strongly!"

Broussard glared at him. "Your protest itself is excessive and unwarranted, considering it was you who brought that bloody-handed spy into my camp!"

"You have no proof against him!" persisted the major. "Only your scout's unsupported word!"

"His word is enough for me!"

"An accusation doesn't constitute evidence! An accused man is deemed innocent until proved guilty by a court of law. You have no right to commit my nephew to brutal punishment! I call upon every fair-minded man here——"

"I'll place you under arrest in a minute!" Broussard threatened. "Insubordination and incitement to mutiny! Aiding an enemy, a spy, a notorious renegade!"

"Blood brother to the Apaches," Soderman put in. "Proof? I wager he wears the sign on his chest. Three cuts, ashes rubbed in, making a black scar like a tattoo mark." He made to rip open the front of Drury's shirt.

Drury stepped back from the reaching fingers. "Never mind that. Let it go."

He heard low murmurs among the onlooking officers. His refusal to have his chest bared counted heavily against him. He saw the beginning of dismayed doubt creep into Major Royal's eyes, and hated to see what must come. Yet he felt a sense of relief that his imposture was ending. He realized how uneasily it had weighed on him, living a lie, hiding under an identity not his own. At first it had seemed a simple expedient, purely temporary. It had become complicated and binding.

He drew a deep breath. "I'm sorry, Major. I'm not your nephew," he said. "Ken Royal died."

"Then you—you're—?"

"My name is Jim Drury."

Major Royal stood rigid. His face paled, then flooded red. He began trembling. His lips moved, but no words came. Words couldn't express his shattered faith, disillusion, the knowledge that one he had trusted and fondly admired was an impostor. The revelation discredited him. His turgid emotions concentrated into rage. Unable to contain himself, he drew his pistol from its holster.

Somebody exclaimed, "No, no, Major!"

For a few seconds Drury looked directly into the muzzle, aware of the major's finger tightening on the trigger. This, he thought, is the end of me. I'll never know what happens at the Chiricahua Stronghold tomorrow. Never have to care.

The pistol stroked upward and slammed down on his head.

CHAPTER THIRTEEN

Arms manacled behind him, chained to a wheel of a supply wagon, he could neither stand up nor lie down. He tried shifting for an easier position. There wasn't any. He could only squat cramped on the ground. His head ached, his throat was parched, and he was miserably cold.

The clink of the chain drew alert inspection from the two troopers on guard over him. No use asking them for a drink, for anything. Broussard would have their hides. Two troopers to guard a chained prisoner. Broussard must have suspected that some of the infantrymen might still stubbornly believe in him and smuggle him a drink.

He hadn't any recollection of being brought here, so he supposed he'd been senseless from the major's wallop. It couldn't have been long ago, maybe a couple of hours, for it was still dark. They'd had to carry him. Or drag him. After, of course, taking his gun and knife. His hat was gone, too.

His face itched as if mites crawled all over the skin. Nothing to do about that, hands fastened behind his back. He let his head loll forward and attempted with will power to shut out pains and discomforts. A stoical Indian trick.

Two men paced in step along the line of wagons and halted near him. Thinking they were relief guards, Drury didn't raise his head until one of them, Sergeant O'Trist, commented woodenly, "I tagged you correct, mister. You're a wrongun."

"Spit on him, Irisher!" said Corporal Lagerfeld. "Call him dirty names! He saved your scalp, is all!"

"It's the reason I'm here. Hand me the canteen."

The two troopers barred them. "Nobody allowed to approach the prisoner, no talking to him, no food or water," droned the older of the two. "General's orders."

"The man's suffering! A little water——"

"No. General's orders."

"To hell with your tinpot general! Get out of our way!"

The troopers brought their carbines up to the ready. "Any you doughfoots try helping this stinkin' renegade, we shoot! General's orders again."

"What's going on here?" Captain Gaylord emerged from the darkness. "Sergeant! Corporal! Are you interfering with my men on duty?"

"They were, sir!" blurted the younger trooper. "They threatened us. They called the general a——"

"T'shun!" cracked the captain, and the two snapped to attention. "About turn!" They about-turned, facing away from the wagon. "I'll inspect the prisoner."

He dropped to one knee and tugged a flask from his pocket. "You're a self-confessed impostor, but I'm not convinced of all the rest of it," he muttered dispassionately. "It doesn't ring true. Tip your head back and open your mouth. Whiskey and water. Don't choke on it."

Drury drank in gulps. Gaylord restored the flask to his pocket and drew out a handkerchief. He motioned silently for the canteen. Corporal Lagerfeld, watching the back-turned troopers, gave it to him. Gaylord soaked the handkerchief and bathed Drury's face and the gash in his head. For such a severe and soured man, he had gentle hands.

"I knew a fellow like you once. Hanged for murder.

They found later he didn't do it. *Are* you a blood brother to the Apaches?"

"Not to the Chiricahuas and allied tribes. I've fought against them."

"He sure has!" Lagerfeld whispered. "My bunch knows it." O'Trist grunted a grudging confirmation.

Gaylord looked searchingly into Drury's eyes. "If I had my way I'd take off your irons. I could use you tomorrow, as guide. How do you rate the prospects?"

"Not good," Drury answered. "The general's plan seems plain stupid to me. I've never seen worse country for cavalry to fight in, and I only saw the edge of it. But Soderman's an expert scout, none better. He could know something I don't. I hope he does."

"He must have good reason to favor the plan. It's probably not as stupid as it seems to you. The cavalry is well able to fight in rough country." A coolness shaded Gaylord's tone. Rising, he nodded dismissal to O'Trist and Lagerfeld. To the two troopers, he said, "At ease. Continue duty."

He strode off without another word, evidently regretting his lapse into befriending a civilian who voiced the preposterous opinion that a bit of rough terrain might obstruct cavalry.

Drury shook his head wearily. Impossible to sway them, even the old captain, despite his long service—or perhaps because of it. They still thought in terms of maneuvering and deploying and the roaring charge. Where they were going there wouldn't be space or opportunity for any sort of extended charging line. They didn't know, couldn't visualize the Chiricahua Stronghold. Well, tomorrow they would learn. There's nothing, he thought, I can do to stop that. Nothing.

But why did Soderman favor the vainglorious plan of attack? It was understandable in Broussard, ignorant of

113

the country and its Indians, opinionated, dazzled by delusions of grandeur. Soderman, though, had years of experience. He had often served as an Army scout and won commendations. He wasn't harebrained, far from it, Drury fell asleep on the problem.

The camp came astir long before daybreak. Officers issued commands, and the noncoms hurried to see to it that they were carried out. Troopers saddled and bridled their mounts in the dark, breathing curses, the animals snuffy at this early hour. Drivers sorted out teams, backed them to wagons, buckled on harnesses. All the orderly hubbub of a mixed Army brigade preparing to march.

Listening to it, Drury figured the noise could be clearly heard at least a mile off in the crisp air. Apache scouts prowling the outer darkness, he imagined, were cocking their ears, perfectly well aware of what was happening. Not that it mattered. The column couldn't march without raising a racket of clopping hoofs and trundling wheels. And when the cavalry units pressed onward, the sound of their horses would advertise their advance. Besides, they'd be spied on all the way.

Yet Broussard proposed to catch the enemy napping. Maybe he believed all Indians were slothful wretches who slept most of the time in a sodden stupor. He may have formed that conclusion after seeing a few reservation drunks and camp moochers. The Apaches would stumble awake in panic when he burst upon them.

Like hell they would. Not unless Soderman and his paid Indian scouts had somehow drugged the whole kit and caboodle of them—a farfetched fancy.

Drury had another fancy, not so farfetched. He wondered if Captain Gaylord would remember, in the busy bustle of duties, to free his chain from the spokes before

114

the forward march began. If not, he could see himself circling over and over, a human pinwheel. The column was shaping up. He heard the cavalrymen leading their mounts to position forward, harried by the gruff barks of noncoms. The infantrymen, today afoot again, formed ranks ahead of the supply wagons. The drivers climbed to their seats and took the lines.

"Captain, don't forget me!"

A buckskinned figure loomed over him. "Cramps?"

"No. Squinching to ride with the wheel."

"The march won't start till I'm ready," Soderman said. "The Gen'l relies on me."

"I noticed you play up to him, feed his vanity." And that was another puzzle. Contempt for high-ranking Army brass was Harl Soderman's trademark.

"The Gen'l's vanity ain't hard to feed. I persuaded him to give you in my charge." Stooping behind Drury, Soderman, with a key, clicked open the padlock on the chain. "How're the legs?"

"They're okay." His wrists stayed manacled behind, the chain dragging.

"Better be! Walk ahead o' me up the line." Soderman picked up the chain, left-handed, his right hand holding a gun. "You'll walk, here on—or trot, or run—to the Stronghold!"

"Why?" Drury aked.

Soderman grinned, only with his narrow lips. "I told the Gen'l they won't shoot, the White Apache leading us in! Now walk—fast!"

Drury walked. Passing the major's light-wheeled ambulance, directly behind the infantrymen, he paused, wanting to speak to the major. The gun at his spine prodded him on.

"Keep walking—you got a long way to go!"

He saw a face peering from between the canvas flaps

of the ambulance. Linley. He couldn't tell what was her expression. Revulsion, pity—only the darkness knew. He didn't want pity. The face receded, though the canvas flaps stayed parted. She was gone. So it must have been revulsion. Hell. Men—men like Jake Lagerfeld, O'Trist, all the others—they stuck by, fart the evidence.

"Keep walking!"

At the head of the column, Broussard, gloved and cockily hatted, inquired, "Ready, Soderman?" He wore a sword, although swords were ruled out-outmoded by order of the War Department. He could not say *Mister* to one he considered an inferior: *Mister* Soderman. He was an arrant snob.

Yet the famed scout responded civilly, "Ready, sir!"

He was mounted on a bay gelding, Drury's chain loop over his right forearm. "We'll reach Point of Rocks before sunup."

"Give the order to mount," Broussard instructed Captain Gaylord impatiently. "Ready to march."

The order went relayed down the line. Saddles creaked and legs thumped leather. The infantrymen resignedly straightened ranks, bullied quietly by Sergeant O'Trist and Corporal Lagerfeld, who seemed to have worked out some sort of understanding between them. The wagon drivers drew up the slack in their lines.

"Forward!"

At Point of Rocks the brigade halted to reshuffle and divide forces. This was the jump-off point for the cavalry. Army chronicles would later record that this was the place of fateful decision for the commanding officer. Here he based his supply train, guarded by infantry.

Well and good. The wagons couldn't proceed farther, anyway, due to impassable terrain—steep and rocky

116

slopes that no wheeled vehicle on earth could navigate.

Here the C.O. divided his cavalry, himself commanding two companies, the remainder angling off under a captain who didn't know the route.

A dubious stratagem. Army historians would wag their heads. By much the same stratagem General George A. Custer, no greenhorn by any means, had come a fearful cropper against the Sioux at the Little Big Horn.

"I'll lead the way, Gen'l," Soderman said. "Ain't no need to put out advance guards, long's I'm ahead. Just keep me in sight."

He hadn't spoken to Drury throughout the march to Point of Rocks. He didn't speak to him until, toiling up the mountain slope, Drury having to trot to keep pace with the bay horse, they were fifty yards forefront of Broussard's cavalry column. Drawing the bay to a walk, he said then, "Dumb bastard! Advance guards are regulation. He don't know soldiering."

"Where are your Indian scouts?" Drury asked him.

"They're around."

"I bet! Like the Chiricahuas. I know they're all round us, watching, waiting."

"You got that same gift, too?" Soderman inquired. "So've I. I can smell an enemy at a mile. I smelled you right away!"

Continuing, he said, "It wouldn't do no good, you call back to the Gen'l. He won't believe a word you say. I'll tell you—this bolo bunch behind us is about to get hashed! You know why I'm telling you."

"Sure. To break me down. Make me squirm." Drury kept his voice calm, matching Soderman's level tone. "You're leading us all into disaster, yes, but why? It can't be just on account of me. I put a bullet in your neck, but that's a personal grudge between us. Nobody sacrifices a brigade," he said reasonably, "to pay off his score against only one man."

"That's right."

"Is it Broussard, too, you hate?"

"You're getting close to it. The Gen'l," Soderman said, "stands for every gold-braid son-of-a-bitch that ever made small of me. Contempted me. I got a funny build. I don't talk good. I stink. They don't invite me to eat with 'em. My Injun scouts' handouts from the commissary, troopers' hardtack . . . Goddam 'em! The Gen'l is a-a-"

"An epitome of white men's arrogance, I grant. An example of gold-braid authority of the worst kind. Still—"

"Well put. You got the words."

"Still, you're a white man yourself."

Soderman expelled a gust of breathy, near-silent laughter. "Me? I'll tell you something more that might break and squirm you. I was taken by Apaches when I was a kid, before I remember. I grew up Apache—a goddam good warrior. I've et equal with Geronimo, Victorio, Nachez. The big men. The leaders. They made me warchief. Me, that don't know my born name! The Apaches respect me, honor me."

"You live a double life," Drury commented. He would not show his horrified dismay. "Part time Army scout, rest of the time Apache."

"It won't be double much longer."

"No, it won't be anything if you betray this brigade!"

"Drury," said Soderman, "you're a snooty paleface like all the rest. You don't understand. This is a war. My people have got ready for it, with my figuring. I know the strength of every Army post in the territory. My people attack where and when I tell 'em to. I've got

118

it all worked out in my head. We'll take all Arizona before summer's over!"

"Then what?"

"I'll be head chief of all the Apaches."

"You won't last. This is federal territory. You'll have the Army on your neck. Pardon the expression."

Soderman shrugged. "Nothing lasts forever. After I bust this Broussard brigade, it'll take the Washington slowpokes a year to put an army in the field. Congressional appropriations. Senate investigations. Wrangling over who should be in command. Then the campaign mapped out and approved . . . A year at least."

"But finally they'll get you," Drury said.

"No, no. Me and my people can always fade off down into Mexico when the going gets bad, and raid from there. The Mexicans couldn't run us out if they tried. By then I'll have all scores paid. I'll have had my day, hundreds of days!"

Drury turned his head to look at the heavy-lidded oyster eyes. "You hate whites that much? You enjoy making them suffer?"

"I'm Apache," was the reply. "The screams are music to me. I hate everybody who ain't a fighting Apache. Like your damn Bloodstoners. Traitors, them. I got special plans for you. Man, what plans! You'll suffer the full measure—three days—wishing every minute you was dead."

"That's four thousand, three hundred and twenty minutes. Can you spare the time?"

"Make it five thousand. You might last, big-strong feller like you. The major's daughter—I saw her. She kinda wrinkled up her nose at me. I got plans for her, too, before I give her to the young bucks. Face front and keep on walking!" Soderman wrenched the chain upward, twisting Drury's manacled arms. With the loose loop of the chain he lashed Drury on the back. "Don't you give me that look!"

Made suddenly furious by Drury's look of contempt, he struck again. He must have seen often the same look in the eyes of white captives. It exasperated him. They couldn't seem to realize his mastery. His grotesque build robbed him of the grand dignity that he always sought.

"I'll break you, Drury! You'll beg for death. Not for mercy—hell, no! For death!" The chain beat Drury's shoulders.

A young lieutenant rode forward from the following cavalry column. "General Broussard requires that you keep this prisoner alive," he stated snappily. "Not beat him dead!"

"I ain't killing him. Just punishing him."

Pinched by rocks on both sides, the trail shrank so narrow that the cavalry troopers had to thread along it in single file, officers walking their horses foremost, the loud stamping of hoofs echoing up the long rise—*clop-clop,* a sound for any ear within a mile or more.

They're all round us, Drury sensed. Can't see them, but they're there. Waiting ready to swamp us, massacre us. And still nothing I can do. Nothing to do to save this brigade, doomed by an incompetent commander.

They toiled to the mountain top, and from there they stared down into an utter impossibility for horsemen—a jungle of immense rocks, nightmare shapes so close together that a man afoot had to squeeze past. And caves and diggings behind every rock. The Chiricahua Stronghold. It extended far in its narrow cleft of valley.

Centuries of erosion had carved the rocks into fantastic forms, some resembling gigantic beasts of a pre-

120

historic era. Huge boulders balanced on pinnacles, seemingly about to topple off although they had rested there for ages. Nature here had played weird pranks with its tools of climate changes, sandstorms, slow erosion, doing the work of mad sculptors.

Nothing grew in the rock and sand, and the overlooking walls of cliffs rose starkly bare. There was no life visible anywhere. The place couldn't support life.

But the caves and pits behind rocks were made by human hands, by men inured to heat, thirst, hunger, able to survive where others perished. The warriors for generations had kept this mountain fastness as their impregnable stronghold, their retreat from raids with plunder and captives. Now it was the main headquarters and supply source for the Apache uprising. They wouldn't let it be taken, Drury was certain.

"What next, Soderman?"

CHAPTER FOURTEEN

Reining in his horse, Soderman didn't reply. He let the chain hang slack. His heavy-lidded eyes flashed wide open for a moment, and he smiled almost like a boy who planned a mischievous joke on his elders.

Drury looked back. The cavalry column was coming up to the crest, fours-abreast squeezed to two-abreast by the trail. A corporal flaunted a guidon, blue and yellow, which hung limply on its staff in the still air. A brave sight, though, the troopers steadily following it, self-assured, unaware of defeat waiting ahead, God help them.

Leading, Broussard halted his white horse level with Soderman on the crest and raised his right hand for the column to halt. He surveyed the terrain down below, dismayed by its inaccessible appearance. He was a showy horseman on a flat parade ground.

"Soderman—what the devil's this? It's uninhabited! The trail down only allows single file! Have you lost your way?"

"No, Gen'l," responded Soderman. "Appearances are sure deceptive from up here. I'll lead you down to the Apaches, and I swear you'll catch 'em napping like you said. It's my job."

"Well . . ." Broussard scanned the steep thread of downward trail anxiously. "Does it get better farther on?"

"No, it gets worse!" Drury said, unable to restrain himself longer. "It's only for Indians on foot—not for horses, any part of it! Your scout's guiding you into an ambush that'll—"

Soderman, on his horse, kicked him on the back of the head. Drury fell onto his face, to the length of the chain, and Broussard said to Soderman, who hauled Drury back up onto his feet, "You could kill him for all I personally care, but I'm officially responsible for him as a federal prisoner. There are witnesses. Two companies."

"Right, Gen'l. Don't worry—I'm saving him for better things. Much better. Slower."

It didn't occur to Broussard to inquire into the meaning of Soderman's response. He was too occupied with scanning the trail. Nor did he spy the defensive diggings. "How far down this sorry excuse for a trail do we have to go?"

"Not far. You might's well give your order to advance, Gen'l, if you don't mind me suggesting, while the enemy don't expect you. Hit 'em before they wake up! Like Gen'l Crook on the Rosebud! Like Custer on the Washita!" The scout didn't mention that those onslaughts had been launched against unsuspecting Sioux slumbering in the dead of winter, north in muffling snow, in their tepees . . .

"Forward!"

Broussard high-armed his gloved and gauntletted hand in a sweeping gesture which, following his spoken command, was rather superfluous and more than a little theatrical. Bringing his hand down, he unsheathed his sword with a grand flourish, doubtless regretting that there weren't any newspaper reporters present to pen in deathless prose the record of his actions for posterity.

The officers and men of the two cavalry companies rode on after him, taking single file on the narrow strip of trail pitching steeply downward to the desolate valley.

Drury's senses twanged. How could they, the riders behind him and Soderman, be so unconscious of danger? They rode stolidly, insensitive, concerned only with their mounts and the tricky difficulties of the trail.

"How far?" Broussard asked Soderman again. He was having trouble with his handsome white horse. It wasn't accustomed to precipitous mountain trails scantly a foot wide, bordered by a sheer drop. Neither was Broussard.

And again Soderman answered him, "Not far, Gen'l!"

Not far. As soon as the two companies of cavalrymen strung out all in single file on the down trail, like target ducks in a shooting gallery, the silently waiting and watching Apaches attacked.

They swarmed from everywhere, on all sides, firing, screeching war-whoops. Being on the fierce offensive, they couldn't abide to huddle sniping from cover. Every warrior hungered to win for himself the scalp and accoutrements of a hated white soldier.

Broussard, eyes bulging, shouted, "Charge!" A senseless order. The troopers were limited by the narrow confines of the trail—as Army historians would gravely indicate later in precise wording. The hostiles attacked all around them. Charge where? Charge how?

Realizing that his cavalry was trapped, outnumbered by the sudden horde, Broussard changed his order to, "Fall back!"

Another senseless order. There wasn't space to turn and retreat, as he discovered when trying to wheel his horse around. The horse balked, panicked. Cavalrymen dismounted without order, crouched, fired their short-barrelled saddle rifles—poverty firearms that fouled the breech in a few shots. Broussard lowered his useless sword.

"Soderman! What the devil's this you've got me into?"

"A jackpot," Soderman replied coolly in the racketting chaos. "You big-mouth bastard," he said in the same tone of voice, and shot Broussard twice in the chest.

"God—!" Broussard slumped off the white horse.

"That's the end of a fool," Soderman murmured, breaking open his gun and extracting the empty shell cases. The troopers and junior officers, fighting for their lives, hadn't noticed the incident.

"A brave fool," Drury said.

He snatched the chain from Soderman's occupied hands and swung its loop at Soderman's head. Soderman ducked fast. The chain, which Drury had to swing awkwardly by spinning himself around, hands manacled behind him, struck the horse. Already made skittish by the uproar, the horse exploded a squeal and took off in bucking jumps, Soderman sawing reins to bring it under control. Missing its footing on a jump, it slid off the edge of the trail, rear end first, pawing frantically like a cat scrambling down a tree trunk.

Drury hoped the fall might break Soderman's neck, but he didn't count on it. That man was much more likely to keep his seat until the horse rolled, then spring clear to take his leading place with the Apache horde.

The cavalry companies lost all semblance of military cohesion. Officers and noncoms shouted orders, trying vainly to impose discipline on catastrophe in a hopeless situation. Broussard's bugler lay dead alongside the corporal who had borne the guidon. Unhorsed men ran back up the trail, jostling one another, the Apaches blazing at them, picking them off. Troopers who had managed to get their horses turned crowded those on foot.

The Apaches, Drury thought, aren't firing at me—because Soderman told them beforehand that he wants me taken alive. He has that much power among them. They do his bidding. They have trust in him.

Here at last was materialization of the old worry that some day the Apache tribes might all unite to rid the country of the hated whites. Obstacles to singleness of purpose had always been jealous prejudices between tribes, differences of tradition, the lack of a guiding mastermind they could all trust. Soderman had accomplished the miracle, spending years to bring it about.

A distant bugle pealed a call, the rapid notes thin and tinny in the gunfire. Through the haze of dust and smoke Drury made out a line of blue-clad horsemen trickling into sight on the far side of the valley. Captain Gaylord's outfit. Hearing the din, Gaylord had quit the lower route and come directly over the hills.

"God, no!" Drury muttered. "It's just more for the slaughter!"

The size of the enemy force must have shocked the captain, for he brushed a hand across his eyes as if hardly believing what he saw—Apache warriors everywhere, Broussard's companies in broken retreat. Yet on his order the bugler again sounded off an urgent call.

More troopers appeared, spurring their mounts after the captain, forming loosely into column on the gallop behind him. For this side of the valley they looked almost toy-like, vulnerable, a comparatively small detachment. Many of the warriors ceased fire to stare, some grunting grim amusement. Those horse soldiers had avoided riding into an ambush set for them farther along the lower route, only to ride into this shambles.

Incredibly, but very apparently, Gaylord intended to attack. Vastly outnumbered, he would launch a charge, on the worst kind of battlefield for cavalry, extended formation out of the question. Drury shook his head. Sheer madness.

Seemingly changing his mind, Gaylord suddenly wheeled off to his left. By that shift he avoided the worst of the maze of rocks, but there was nowhere he could find room to spread out his men. If, Drury thought, that was what he sought.

It wasn't. The detachment came circling on around, in column of twos, Gaylord at the head. The bugle sounded once more, and the troopers fired on the dead run. Then they were thundering along the foot of the slope below the trail, still in twos, wielding their carbines as clubs.

It wasn't madness. Drury felt a swell of admiration for the calculated audacity. Captain Gaylord hadn't intended any foolhardy frontal attack, only feinted at it. His purpose was to cut a passage through the enemy, his troopers striking closely pair-after-pair like a jackhammer at one spot. To do it, that old veteran captain must have instilled in the troopers a deep respect for him, an unquestioning faith in his leadership.

They couldn't be stopped, the rag-tag of Apaches at the foot of the slope dodging the smashing sweep of carbines and charging line of horses. The Apache warriors had probably never before known of such a thin-piercing cavalry maneuver, cavalry being famous for the frontal charge, guidons fluttering, at 'em and be damned to the odds. This?

Many years later, great armies, highly mobile, would

copy the same tactics. A slice-through, concentrated on a single point, to disorganize the foe. Not a line of credit to Captain Gaylord in the record.

Well, he didn't invent anything new. Charioteers of the Roman legions had employed comparable tactics.

Where the trail dipped low toward its end, Gaylord wheeled his detachment onto it, the troopers falling into single file, and came cantering up. His soured face, unexcited, showed only an added severity. He reined in his horse, glancing at Drury and on upward at the pandemonium of men and horses as if coldly weighing a problem.

"Did I see Soderman down there among the hostiles?"

"You did!" said Drury. "He planned this trap. He's on their side. He gunned Broussard down."

The captain twitched his nose, but made no comment. He looked back and rapped, "Reload and fire at will, fast! We cover the retreat of those men up there!"

The Apaches were reassembling, furious at the success of his maneuver. Young braves dashed forward to attempt clambering up the steep slope, to get hand-to-hand with him and his troopers. In the tumult of warwhoops and gunfire Drury thought he heard the voice of Soderman repeatedly shouting an order, trying to restrain the maddened young braves. Soderman had miscalculated on the ambushing of Gaylord's column along the lower route, and didn't want heavy casualties to count against him as a result of it. He couldn't afford costly mistakes.

Dismounting, Gaylord rummaged in a pocket, produced the key to Drury's manacles, and unlocked them. "You might find a gun nobody's using," he said with bitter dryness. Dead men and firearms littered the trail.

His sour exterior cloaked a human concern for men under him.

Broussard's white horse, trained to a hair, stood trembling, not moving from the spot where its master had tumbled off. Drury took its reins. He bent over Broussard, unbuckling and stripping off his pistol and belt—a Colt's single action .44, handsomely engraved, fitted with pearl grips. Swank, like the horse, like the sword, but a dependable gun.

Broussard stirred, rolling his face over on the ground. He stared glazedly up at Captain Gaylord. "Soderman —shot me!" he mumbled.

The captain, firing down the slope, nodded impassively. "When we pull the command out of this hell-hole . . ." He glanced at the staring eyes. "He's gone. What's on your mind, Drury?"

"The supply wagons back at Point of Rocks," Drury replied. "Soderman won't have overlooked them."

"They're probably under attack now. What could you do about it? That is, assuming you got there," Gaylord said between shots. "You can't even cram past the retreat until you get over the . . ." He broke off, having a thought. "Oh. Yes, of course. Major Royal's daughter."

"Soderman told me he had special plans for her."

"Oh," Gaylord said again. "Well, then." He blew acrid powdersmoke from his nostrils with a snort. "Good luck to you, this evil day."

"Same to you."

"Uh-huh. You were right—this is no place for cavalry. But we'll get out of it somehow, what's left of us."

"The wounded—"

"We'll do what we can for them. Our dead we'll have

to leave behind. Token of defeat. Total defeat, caused by stupidity!"

"Not total, Captain," Drury contradicted. "Soderman planned an all-out massacre. You broke that plan."

CHAPTER FIFTEEN

The supply train looked as if a hurricane had struck it. Canvas tops hung torn. The teams were gone from the roped-in corral. The infantrymen huddled under the wagons, tending to injured while keeping tense lookout.

"A band of 'em ripped right through us," Corporal Lagerfeld told Drury. "Quiet as ghosts, before they stampeded the teams. You never saw action so fast."

He had brightened at Drury's arrival, until he took note of his expression and the horse he rode.

"How's it with the cavalry?" he asked somberly.

"Smashed," Drury said. "They're straggling back here. Where's Major Royal?"

"Gone searching for his daughter."

"Searching for—? Jake, tell it to me straight! What happened here?"

"They broke into the ambulance and carried her off." Lagerfeld spread his hands. "It was fast, everything popping all at once. Then they were gone. The major was down the other end of the line. He went limping after 'em."

"You let him go alone?"

"Let him? You don't argue with a commanding officer, 'specially with a gun in his hand! Guess he forgot what he was, though. So did O'Trist. He followed the major, leaving me to hold the bunch together for the next attack." Lagerfeld wagged his head. "Properly speaking, they're both deserters. Left their posts. Won't matter when the Apaches catch 'em."

"Which way did they go?"

"Roughly west. You going too?"

"Sure!" Drury said. "First I need spare shells for this gun, and a rifle."

Lagerfeld gestured, sighing. "There's an arms and ammunition wagon. Take what you want. I ain't the quartermaster. My friend—"

"H'm?"

"I hate to see you go. If you find that Irisher alive, give him a kick in the pants for me."

When Drury left the forted-in supply train, Corporal Lagerfeld raised his right hand briefly in a farewell wave that verged on a sketchy sort of slaute.

Besides being dangerously conspicuous, the white horse wasn't at its best in rough country. A parade horse, ill-chosen for harsh duty, it grew fretful at Drury's style of riding and the demands he put upon it.

And this country was rough, harsh—broken ridges of red rimrock, one after another, interspersed by sandy hollows. Farther on it appeared to worsen, the ridges running closer together as if some mighty convulsion had squeezed them like the bellows of a concertina. They ended against a high, miles-long cliff, an escarpment, the face of it gashed by deep clefts that Mexicans called *barrancos*.

Reading trail sign in sandy patches—two sets of boot prints superimposed on the tracks of moccasins—Drury judged that he wasn't far behind Major Royal and the sergeant. Nor were the Apaches any great distance ahead. He hoped the pair wouldn't stumble on them before he caught up.

He had seen where the band of warriors had split soon after raiding the supply train, one party cutting off northward, probably to rejoin the main force. The prints of Linley's shoes showed among the tracks of the rest. Her captors weren't hurrying, nor covering their

132

trail. They didn't expect any serious pursuit from the foot soldiers, and were confident that the cavalry by now had perished in Soderman's trap. The white rule was shattered. This was the Red Year.

Drury dismounted and loosened the saddle a notch. The white horse had become a hazard and a hindrance.

He headed it back the way it had come and started it with a slap on the rump. It might or might not have the gumption to retrace its route to the supply train.

He hung the rifle to his shoulder by its sling and pressed on, making better time on foot when climbing the ridges. God only knew where the Apaches were taking Linley. To some prearranged destination, he supposed. A private hideout, dictated by Soderman, there to be held until he came for her, or sent for her.

He sighted Major Royal and the sergeant toiling up a ridge, the major hobbling, a hand leaning on O'Trist's solid shoulder. He didn't dare raise a hail to them. They paused at the top to peer beyond, and crossed on over, taking only the barest precaution. He listened, then hurried after them, his long legs carrying him in leaping bounds down one ridge and up another.

Fools. Two brave fools, Linley's father, wounded, and a self-appointed guardian whose devotion outweighed his brains. Old soldiers, they scarcley knew the rudiments of the art of stalking, but they were stumbling to rescue her from Indians as alert and ferocious as wildcats.

He came upon them halted in a sandy hollow, the major down on one knee, O'Trist bent worriedly over him. They didn't hear Drury approach until he said quietly, "Major, you're about done in."

O'Trist whirled, eyes bulging, instantly angry at having been caught off guard. "Who let you loose?"

"Hold your voice down. It was Captain Gaylord, during the retreat."

"What retreat?"

Drury had forgotten that they hadn't learned the disastrous outcome of Broussard's cavalry campaign. Rapidly and tersely, he told them of it, and of Soderman's part in it. The major's face, sweating with pain and fatigue, grayed.

"His whole command—wiped out?"

"I think not, as long as the captain's alive. If any man can pull it together, he can. He's fighting a retreat back to the supply train, or he was when I left."

"Heavy losses?"

"Not as heavy as could've been. Soderman planned it for a massacre. He didn't get it. The Apaches took losses, too, mostly from Captain Gaylord's detachment. But it's a defeat for us, no good saying it's not."

"You ran out on it?" O'Trist queried, then flushed, muttering, "I take that back."

"I left with the captain's permission," Drury said. "Not that I needed it, not tied to the Army. I had to find out what might've happened to the supply train. I found out, and I'm here."

He stepped around Sergeant O'Trist and booted him on the backside. "Compliments of Jake Lagerfeld."

The sergeant lowered his ready fists. "Huhn," he grunted, understanding. "Okay."

Major Royal looked at Drury's head. "About that blow I struck you with my gun. I was—well, call it disappointed, though that doesn't cover it by far. I'd come to regard you almost like a son. Then, when you admitted being a liar and imposter—"

"I understand, sir."

"Just one question. Did you kill my nephew and rob him of his papers of identity?"

"No," Drury answered. "He got an Apache bullet. Days later, dying, he urged me to take his identity for long enough to get clear. Because I was outlawed, wanted. Still am."

"He must have believed in you." The major struggled laboringly to his feet. "Got to move on!"

"No, you stay here."

"I'm going on! My daughter's in the hands of a pack of filthy savages!"

"Jayzus!" growled O'Trist. "They'll—"

"They won't do anything bad to her," Drury stated.

"What makes you think that?"

"Yes, what?"

The two old soldiers, major and sergeant, stared at him. He drew a long breath and let it out, to quell impatience. Explanations irritated him, especially explanations of what seemed to him obvious and reasonable.

"They're holding her for Soderman," he said. "We're close to 'em. Fourteen warriors. Grown men. They've made a halt."

"How d'you know?" O'Trist challenged.

"Because I read sign. Because they can't climb up that cliff. Because Soderman wouldn't have trusted the job to any wild young bucks—they get out of hand. They'd leave a mutilated corpse for him, the young bucks. He'd lose out on the fun."

Major Royal shuddered. "Linley—!"

"So the fourteen ahead of us are older warriors," Drury continued. "Dependable. Personally picked by Soderman. There are three of us. Do we charge in? Repeat Broussard's blunder?"

"Your brain's working," O'Trist acknowledged. "Fetch up an idea. We ain't leaving Missy where she is, that's for damn sure!"

"I propose to scout forward and see what's what.

You stay here with the major. Keep your ears and eyes sharp."

O'Trist frowned, taking the injunction as an oblique criticism. "How 'bout it we creep up on 'em, get the drop—"

"Not a hope. Even if we could, they'd kill Linley before they let her go. Rest that leg, Major."

Between the last ridge and the cliff, the gap ran wide and crooked like a ditch dug by drunks without particular purpose. A tiny trickle of water, drainage from the cliff, threaded through the gap. Stunted brush grew along the course of the trickle—stunted because of intermittent drouth years when there was no drainage.

The clefts in the cliff, the *barrancos,* debouched into the gap. Some of them, oddly graceful with smoothly rounded edges, resembled the folds of a flowing Spanish skirt. One, partly encircled by a fold of sandstone sparkling with silica, had a beaten footpath leading up the low bank to its entrance.

For perhaps two hours of the day, or less, the blazing sun in its overhead arc shone into the gap. The rest of the day the gap lay shaded, cool while the earth outside baked. The gap was in shade now, the sun sinking in its late afternoon phase. The fourteen warriors rested on the low bank, near the cleft that had the footpath leading into it.

They sat in a circle, knees drawn up, arms folded on knees, head bowed at rest on forearms, rifles beside them. Silent images. Always, at every opportunity, Apaches conserved their stamina. They could maintain that cramped position for hour after hour, seemingly slothful and drugged with sleep, then spring alive to perform tremendous feats of strength and endurance.

They had eaten, and had fed the captive white

136

woman, for Soderman wanted her kept healthy for him. She sat in the middle of the silent circle. They hadn't bound her. Didn't need to. The slightest sound would jerk them up. Their keen ears were sentinals. Fleet-footed, they could easily catch her if she tried a dash for freedom. She sat with her hands crossed on her knees, head erect, stoical, prim-like, a young lady in dire adversity but not spirit-broken. Not yet.

Drury lingered his gaze on her, wishing he could let her know of his presence. He couldn't. The warriors would sense it. He had to cool his mind, get loose, detached, think of the situation as merely an unemotional problem. That took effort. It took all the will-power he had learned from the Bloodstone people in Mexico, people whose devout Christianity, couples amicably to an ancient tribal religion on the side, made them masters of self-discipline.

He withdrew noiselessly from the broken top of the overlooking ridge and crept back to the hollow.

"Fourteen seasoned warriors," he said. "They're camped by the mouth of a barranco."

"A what?" Major Royal asked, not knowing a word of Spanish, any more than did Sergeant O'Trist.

Again Drury had to explain, feeling as if he were teaching children in the wilderness. "A deep notch in the cliff, caused by erosion—sandstorms, rainshed from the north mountains, all that, hundreds of years. I guess the Apaches have used it a long time. A cache for supplies, loot, whatever. They've got caches all over this country."

"My daughter?"

"She's all right. I saw her. She'll be all right till Soderman comes. I don't look for him to show up today." Drury stretched himself out on the sand, composing himself physically and mentally in preparation for what was to come.

The major and the sergeant glared outragedly at him. He said to them wearily, "There's not a goddam thing we can do in daylight. Us three against fourteen? Use your heads! They'd slaughter us!"

"Do we stand off?" O'Trist crackled, throat dry. "Listen to her screams?"

"No," Drury said. "We wait here for nightfall. Be quiet. Let me figure a plan."

"Plan, balls!"

"Quiet!"

"Let him be!" Major Royal commanded the sergeant. "He's all we have to depend on!"

"A stinkin' renegade!"

"Quiet!"

"I think I've got it," Drury said. "O'Trist, you're a bastard."

"What?"

"I dare you to follow me tonight."

"You're on!"

"Bueno." Drury closed his eyes. *"Bueno* to hell, Sergeant!"

They crawled to the top of the last ridge. Behind them the coming moon spread paleness into the blue-black night sky. They hugged the ground closely, not daring to skyline themselves. The warriors still squatted motionless, Linley in their midst. The chill of night would presently drive them to seek cover and light a fire, a skimpy Indian fire over which they would jostle for prestigious position, if not for warmth.

Drury nudged O'Trist, before he prowled off, halting beyond the first bend of the gap. A thrown stone wouldn't do. The Apaches were wise to that stale trick.

He took off his hat and rolled it down into the gap. It made soft sounds, barely audible. He eased back to O'Trist and found Major Royal with him. He hadn't thought the major was able to climb so quietly, with his injured leg.

The Apaches were on their feet, listening, rifles held ready. They had heard the soft sounds, but were uncertain of the cause. A jackrabbit, perhaps. If so, further softly skipping sounds should soon follow. None came.

One of the party, evidently the leading warrior, gave a mute signal. They were extraordinarily vigilant even for Apaches. Possibly they sensed an enemy presence. Three of them glided to the bend, peering around it. They couldn't miss seeing the hat lying there in the gap. They froze still, then motioned back to the others.

The leading warrior gave another signal. He and eight more trod noiselessly to the bend, leaving two to guard the captive. The two grasped Linley's arms, pulling her onto her feet. Swiftly, they looped a rawhide rope around her, drew it tight, knotted it. The girl began a cry of pain. It earned her a blow on the head, flat-handed, that silenced her. The two guards shoved her stumbling before them up the footpath to the mouth of the barranco.

Drury expelled a sigh of dismay. The hat trick was a failure. He had hoped by it to draw all the warriors off. But they were too crafty.

He should have known, he thought; should have foreseen this. These were experienced warriors, picked by Soderman to guard his prize for him. They knew all the tricks. They wouldn't go all surging off to an alarm, like brash young braves.

The only hope left was a forlorn hope. Twelve Apaches sidling on beyond the bend only fifty steps away, two shoving Linley onward to prison-security in the cramped-mouthed cleft.

"Cover for me!" he whispered. "Stop the bunch from getting back!"

"You're crazy!" grunted O'Trist. "We can't—"

"Try!"

CHAPTER SIXTEEN

He rose and pounced down the incline. The first three leaping strides landed with slight noise. On the fourth, Drury's foot dislodged a rock that tumbled crunching before him. It had looked to be a solid outcrop. He didn't have time to inspect it in the deepening darkness.

Linley's two gurads whipped around on the footpath. Drury's plunging impetus carried him to them, and they by instinctive reaction jumped apart from his rush. His rifle butt clubbed one in the midriff and jack-knifed him, gurgling. With the barrel, Drury straight-armed the other high on the forehead.

The stomach-damaged one let out a quivering howl, whereupon those down the gap, examining the hat, immediately sped back. O'Trist's rifle and Major Royal's pistol drove them back to cover behind the shoulder of the bend.

Not for long. Wise in warfare, counting enemy shots, the Apaches advanced, swarming around the bend, while Major Royal and Sergeant O'Trist reloaded. They blazed through the gap.

"Chree-christ!" said Drury to Linley, huddling her under his arm. "We've got to take to the barranco!"

"Anything you say, Ken—Jim, I mean. Have they got us?"

"Not yet! They won't get *you!*"

"Not alive? I can't bear hurt, pain. Promise?"

"I promise." He bore her on to the cleft.

Major Royal plunged down the ridge. His leg buckled and he rolled to the bottom, but kept his pistol.

Prone, intent on helping Drury, he fired at the oncoming warriors, drawing their fire upon himself. He might have done better to stay up on the ridge, sniping. Two shots, and the pistol clicked empty. He began the task of reloading.

O'Trist, shooting, scrambled down to him. To the Apaches it must have seemed like the forefront of a mass attack, they dodged back behind the shoulder of the bend to await the onslaught. O'Trist hauled the major upright, and, having nowhere better to go, rushed him across the gap.

Drury, pushing Linley into the barranco, found that it was up to him to cover for the major and the sergeant, instead of they for him. A fast turnabout. From his higher ground he glimpsed the huddle of Apaches crouched below the bend, and he triggered his rifle at them to keep them there. He aimed low, with half-grudging charitableness. They were fighters doing their job. The rights and wrongs of redmen and white couldn't ever be settled by bullets in the guts, or by torture of captives. Cruelty begat cruelty. Savage brutality only led to worse savagery. The Apaches—the Tineh, the People, as they still called themselves—had once been peaceful farmers before the coming of the white scourge.

Drury shot low and sparely. My brothers. Red or any color of skin, my brothers by the grace of God. I have lived among them. Shared food. Smoked with them at grave council fires. They could be most grave, serenely intelligent. Until mad emotion took hold of them. As now, the Red Year. Now they were ravaging savages. Well, white men, too, with less reason, stormed into brutal warfare.

The major and the sergeant came struggling up the path, hugged together like Siamese twins. The sergeant had caught a bullet high on his left shoulder, close to his neck, and was bleeding. The major had got another wound in his unlucky leg, above the knee, forcing him to hop.

Drury waved them on past him into the barranco. A final shot, and he followed them in, reloading his rifle, keeping watch on the rock-warped entrance.

O'Trist struck a match. Its light exposed a cleft that tapered backward into solid rock. Above, the night sky was a narrow, triangular slice, blue-black, brightly star-studded as if seen from the bottom of a well. The empty floor, fairly level, showed scuffs and indentations, signs of the cleft's usage in the past as a cache for arms and supplies for the planned uprising. No doubt many other caches existed, contributed to over the years, secretly, for this Red Year of revolt.

A bullet ricocheted off the crooked entrance and rattled into the barranco. O'Trist hastily dropped the lighted match. "Saints, we've got ourselves in a hellish hole here! What'll we do?" His pinched and shaking voice betrayed an ingrained horror of confined places, more than any fear of death.

"We hold them off from coming in at us," Drury said. "That's all we can do."

"How long?"

"God knows. I don't." The question was senseless, an indication of the burly sergeant's ragged nerves. "Linley, get back behind us and stay low."

"Saints, this hole is—is—"

"Pull yourself together, Sergeant!" Major Royal rapped, not comprehending the man's horror. "If we die, we die!"

"I ain't scared of that, sir. But I dread caves and the like."

"Claustrophobia? You'll have to bear with it. Don't

go to pieces. We can hold out here as long—" The major fired at a shapeless blur in the entrance. A gasp, and the blur vanished. "As long as we have ammunition. Food and water is a different matter. Eh, Drury?"

"Especially water." Wounded men developed raging thirsts. Drury had brought a small canteen of water from the supply strin. He gave it to him. "We've got to go sparing with this. One swallow each, no more. You take charge of it."

"Here they come!" O'Trist said in a normal voice, the need for urgent action overriding his nerves.

The rush of the Apaches, unseen, made only a light patter until the foremost of them darkened the mouth of the barranco, suddenly uttering ear-splitting yells to strike terror into the defenders.

The three men blazed into them, almost point blank, without having to sight their firearms. A warrior fell, another on top of him, choking the little passage. At once, they were dragged out by their feet. The mouth of the barranco cleared empty. The yells broke off. As swiftly as it had come, the rush ceased. Powdersmoke curled upward, caught in the air-draft of the barranco. After the din, the silence was ringing.

"We scorched 'em!" O'Trist gloated. He cleaned and reloaded his rifle in the darkness by long-trained feel, contentedly occupied. Then, his task done, the silence got to him. His abnormal phobia returned. "Now's the chance to break out of here!"

Drury shook his head pityingly. "They had to try us. They won't do that again, but they're on the watch, figuring their next move. We'd sure die if we quit this cover."

"That's your opinion! Me, I'm game to—"

"Ah, use your head! The major can't walk. That

144

wound in your shoulder will soon stiffen it. And there's Linley to think of. Her shoes are worn out."

"I've had to take them off, Sarge," Linley confessed in a small, apologetic voice. "They hurt my feet."

"I could carry—"

"Stay where you are, Sergeant," siad the major. "That's an order."

After a moment O'Trist responded tautly, "Yes, sir. Can I have some water?" The major handed him the canteen, and he took a mouthful from it, drinking it slowly. "God, what I'd give for whiskey now!"

"Pass the canteen to Linley."

"I don't need it yet," Linley said. "The Apaches gave me water. They were strangely careful of me, in a way."

Saving her, Drury thought, but didn't say so, for Soderman. Keeping her healthy and whole, within limits of forced travel. She wouldn't be able to fit those ruined shoes back onto her blistered feet. Wouldn't ever require footwear again if she fell into Soderman's hands. A sinister rumor had long persisted that the elusive White Apache was guilty of cannibalism along with his other hideous crimes. A depraved monster whose captives never escaped to describe his appearance, never.

A volley of rifle fire crashed outside. Here was the next move of the party of warriors, a drastic move endangering the girl as much as the three white men with her. Unable to shoot directly into the barranco, because of its crooked outlet, the warriors took for target the inward-curved shoulders of sandstone, for the benefit of indiscriminate ricochets.

Misshapen bullets and bits of bullets hailed buzzing and droning into the barranco. The prolonged volley ended. The Apaches couldn't possibly continue such rapid fire. Again came the ringing hush.

"Anyone hit?" Drury asked. Receiving negative

murmurs, he said, "They'll come up now to find out what damage they've done to us."

"You said they wouldn't rush us again!" O'Trist rasped at him. "Now you say—"

"This won't be a rush. A feeler. Don't cross me, damn you! Wish I had Jake here!"

That amounted to an insult, yet O'Trist unexpectedly blurted, "Pretty good soldier, that Jew."

"Jake keeps his head."

"That's for damn sure. What d'you want me to do?"

"Stay back. Keep cool. It's only a hole in a cliff. I've seen a thousand. So've you."

In the quietness, Drury crawled to the mouth of the barranco and risked a look outside. Up along the path lean figures advanced stealthily, making no sound whatever. He had his rifle pointed beneath him, haphazardly, and he triggered it off and quickly withdrew. Shots whipped the spot where the flash of his rifle had showed.

He crawled back, saying, "That'll let 'em know we're still alive and got our eyes open." More than that he couldn't promise. A leaden fatalism, pessimism, suddenly oppressed him. Was there any use in fighting on? If he didn't die here, he'd die on a hangrope.

The firing of the Apaches became spasmodic, solitary shots that weren't repeated and presently stopped altogether. A dangerous sign. They were preparing another move. Perhaps the leading warrior had got killed in the first rush, and they were electing the next.

As if reading Drury's bleak mood, Major Royal said in the quiet period, "Jim Drury, tell Linley what you told me. About her cousin, my nephew. Ken Royal. Tell her, Jim."

"What's the use?"

"Tell her! She wants to believe in you. Maybe we

146

won't live till morning. Dammit, don't rob her of—"
The major's voice faltered—"of a little happiness."

Drury moved back to Linley and told her, adding details which he hadn't told the major. About his life with the isolated segment of Christian Apaches, the Bloodstone people, in Mexico. His return north to his homeland with warning of the uprising. His arrest. Kenneth Royal's death.

She leaned against him. "That song you sang to me. Sing it again, Jim."

"Soft in my heart . . ."

She joined her voice to his, following the melody and the well-remembered words. The major nodded, smiling. O'Trist bowed his shaking head, incredulous that they could quietly sing together in this hell-hole. What the keenly watching and listening Apaches thought of it was beyond imagination.

The third move was a coupling of the two previous moves. A fast-shooting charge at the barranco, no furtiveness whatever, the way the whites did it with usual success.

It failed for the only reason that the cramped entrance allowed only two to crowd in at a time. The guns of the defenders blasted them. The warriors withdrew, barking cries of rage, dragging out their dead and wounded. Once more the shooting into the entrance commenced.

"Another attack like that, we'll be out of ammo," the major observed, filling the chambers of his pistol.

"They're running low, too," Drury said. "Notice they fire slower."

"Now's the time!" O'Trist urged. "Let's break out!"

"Shut up!" Major Royal commanded. "Outside, three shots, we're dead!"

Drury went back to Linley. She fell asleep on his shoulder, as serenely as if all troubles were solved by his close presence. In a while he heard the arrival of new-comers outside. A voice cracked an order in the Apache tongue, and the firing stopped.

God Almighty, he thought, recognizing the voice, it's Soderman himself!

Linley stirred on Drury's shoulder, murmuring sleepily, "I'm terribly thirsty."

He reached and took the canteen from Major Royal. There wasn't much left in it, its capacity only a pint-and-half, the regulation size set by some Department brain—twenty-four ounces of water per man per twenty-four hours' active duty. He tilted her head back and trickled the tepid water into her mouth.

CHAPTER SEVENTEEN

"Where are you going?" the major asked.

"To the stream below, for water," Drury answered him.

"You'll get killed! I forbid it!"

"Major," Drury said, "You can't forbid me. I'm a free citizen. Dawn's coming. We can't go through the day without some water. Food, hunger—we can bear that. Tighten up the belt, gnaw leather, eat your boots. Thirst, no! I know what I'm talking about, dammit!"

He crawled on outside and on down the path to the tiny stream. Filling the canteen, he heard a slight noise and instantly slid out his gun.

"You don't dare shoot me!" Soderman's whisper reached him. "I'm all that keeps you alive!"

"The hell!"

"You know it's so! You're low on ammo. Me dead, then what? My braves will slaughter the four of you." Soderman parted brush to peer grinning at Drury. "Send the girl out to me! Price of your life! Her screams—"

Drury fired, missed. He raced back into the barranco. Soderman jeered after him, "You sure think a heap of her! Fine! Wait'll she screams—I want you alive to hear her!"

In the barranco Drury said, "Soderman's got here sooner than I figured. Only a few braves came with him. I don't know what to make of that. In reason, his place is at the head of the main Apache force attacking at Point of Rocks. Unless the supply train is already captured, God forbid!"

"Is it possible he lost prestige in the Chiricahua Stronghold?" suggested the major. "His promised massacre failed there, you say. The Apaches took losses. Perhaps they turned against him—if Captain Gaylord reached the supply train and organized a strong defense."

"Let's pray you're right. They've got no use for a loser, that's a fact. Listen! He keeps calling out to stop shooting. He doesn't want Linley killed."

"The warriors don't seem to obey him much."

"They're impatient to finish us and move on." The firing gradually ceased. Drury listened to the Apache voices. "They're arguing with him. He's telling them to starve us out, smoke us out. Alive. They don't want to spend the time."

"Nor me!" grunted Sergeant O'Trist. "I'll kill that bastard!"

Drury tripped him sprawling. "Soderman's the only control on them! And his control is touch-and-go. If you killed him, they'd slaughter us! Use sense!"

"Be damned to your sense!"

O'Trist bounded up and plunged out, firing his rifle.

He must by chance have hit a warrior, for a short cry rang out. A flurry of shots cracked. There was the sound of the sergeant tumbling down the path, his fallen rifle clattering, then the Apache yelps.

"Oh, Sarge—Sarge!" Linley mourned.

Early dawn paled the mouth of the barranco. Furtive activity rustled there like the scampering of packrats. Fire flamed suddenly, sizzling, bringing Drury to his feet, tearing off his coat. Burning brush gushed smoke billowing at him. He flapped his coat at it, calling to Linley and the major, "Get back as far as you can and stay low!"

150

Ignoring the injunction, Major Royal shed his coat and added its fanning to Drury's. After the first onrush of choking smoke, the fire defeated its own purpose, its heat creating a rising draft that sucked smoke and sparks up through the high crevice as if in a chimney.

Soderman, evidently unaware of the effect, shouted, "You ready to come out?"

"Hell, no!" Drury answered. "We're all right!" He and the major held their coats up to deflect the heat. The fire began dying down. He heard Soderman order the warriors to pile on more brush, but their patience was ended.

Exasperated by the long delay, they refused outright to do his bidding. He cursed them.

"He's fast losing control over them," Drury said. "They resent him. They're in a hurry to finish us and be on their way. One of them sounds like he's blaming him for a brother's death."

Soderman again rapped an order, trying to reassert his waning leadership, even threatening them. Snarling voices reviled him. There was a sharp clack of metal striking metal, and sounds of a brief struggle. A shot thudded. Soderman came tottering in backward, his thick, short legs plowing through the remains of the fire, scattering its embers.

He twisted around, falling heavily, and dragged himself onward. Fire spots smoldered in his buckskins. He raised his face off the ground, staring at Drury, at the major, at Linley, his eyes bewildered as if he wasn't conscious of how he had got there. Two Apaches crowded part way in after him, firing into the thinning smoke, Drury triggered a shot that drove them back, coughing.

The gunfire apparently brought realization to Soderman. He rolled over cumbersomely and sat up, grimacing, pressing a hand to his stomach. "Goddam 'em!" he growled. "Knifed an' shot me in the guts! Shoved me in the fire. Me! My own braves!"

"They're not yours now," Drury said. "You lost."

"I'm not the first great man to lose by a fluke "

"A great man? You? Murderer, torturer, and worse, laying your crimes to me!"

"I was a great man among my Apaches! I won't die humble!" Soderman turned, stiff-necked, to look at Drury. "Don't shoot me," he muttered, fumbling out his gun. He peeled off his buckskin jacket and flannel shirt, and threw them onto the embers of the fire. "You do the same. It'll make more smoke to blind 'em for a while."

Smoldering, the clothing gave off thick smoke, through which the sunlit entrance was a gray blur. The interior of the barranco lay shadowed. Soderman sank back flat on the ground, scratching his bared chest. Sniping came only sparingly from outside, and presently ceased on a shrill yell.

"They're quitting," Soderman said. "Enemy approaching."

Soon, a single volley of gunfire rattled. Moments passed before shapes loomed up beyond the smoke. A voice called into the barranco, "Anyone alive in there?"

"Cover your face and move fast, Captain," responded Major Royal. "It's fairly clear back here."

Captain Gaylord strode in quickly, calling behind him, "Rake this fire out." To the major, he said matter-of-factly, "It was the smoke that guided us. Then the shots. We had to leave our horses back a way. Glad to find you alive, sir. And your daughter. And you, Drury. Who's this? Well—our famous scout!"

152

Soderman opened his eyes. "Famous is right! I'm the White Apache, the genuine article!" he said with pride.

Gaylord nodded. "We know. Many of us saw you on the enemy side, at the Chiricahua Stronghold and later at Point of Rocks, directing their movements."

"How did it go at the supply train?" Drury asked.

"We were able to rally our forces there and hold off the hostiles. I think then Soderman must have lost command, because they became disorganized, breaking up into separate bands. Finally they retreated back toward the Chiricahua Stronghold."

"That's the trouble," Soderman mumbled. "Setbacks discourage 'em. The chiefs get to squabbling, and the whole thing falls apart. I came damn near being king of the Apache nation!" He scratched the tattooed sign on his chest. "You won't see me hang. I don't have long to go. Well, I've had my fun . . ."

His use of the word, fun, sickened Drury, knowing what frightful atrocities it involved. The man was utterly without conscience, incapable of remorse.

The fire had been raked out. Drury helped Linley to her feet and out of the barranco into morning sunshine. Troopers carried out the major and Soderman.

"I'll write out a statement and get Soderman to sign it before he dies," Gaylord told Drury. "There's not much doubt, though, that you'll be arrested. You'll probably have to stand trial in a federal court."

"I expect so," Drury agreed. Beside him, Linley paled.

"However, you'll have plenty of friends on your side," Gaylord went on. "Character witnesses, at least. We'll fight any charge against you. Nobody can guarantee a total acquittal, of course. For instance, impersonating a federal marshal. If that happens to come out, and you're found guilty—"

"What would be his sentence?" Linley asked.

The captain had no idea, but he answered without cracking a smile, "Not more than a hundred years."

"I'll wait," she said.

L(eonard) L(ondon) Foreman was born in London, England in 1901. He served in the British army during the Great War, prior to his emigration to the United States. He became an itinerant, holding a series of odd jobs in the western States as he traveled. He began his writing career by introducing his most widely known and best-loved character, Preacher Devlin, in "Noose Fodder" in *Western Aces* (12/34), a pulp magazine. Throughout the mid thirties, this character, a combination gunfighter, gambler, and philosopher, appeared regularly in *Western Aces*. Near the end of the decade, Foreman's Western stories began appearing in Street & Smith's *Western Story Magazine*, where the pay was better. Foreman's first Western novels began appearing in the 1940s, largely historical Westerns such as *Don Desperado* (1941) and *The Renegade* (1942). The *New York Herald Tribune* reviewer commented on *Don Desperado* that "admirers of the late beloved Dane Coolidge better take a look at this. It has that same all-wool-and-a-yard-wide quality." Foreman continued to write prolifically for the magazine market as long as it lasted, before specializing exclusively for the book trade with one of his finest novels, *Arrow in the Dust* (1954) which was filmed under this title the same year. Two years earlier *The Renegade* was filmed as *The Savage* (Paramount, 1952), the two are among several films based on his work. Foreman's last years were spent living in the state of Oregon. Perhaps his most popular character after Preacher Devlin was Rogue Bishop, appearing in a series of novels published by Doubleday in the 1960s. George Walsh, writing in *Twentieth Century Western Writers*, said of Foreman: "His novels have a sense of authority because he does not deal in simple characters or simple answers." In fact, most of his fiction is not centered on a confrontation between good and evil, but rather on his characters and the changes they undergo. His female characters, above all, are memorably drawn and central to his stories.